# Che



# Crime

## Book One

## A Laurel London Mystery

## Tonya Kappes

For my guys!

I love you!

## Chapter One

"Thank God you're here," I hollered to Derek Smitherman who had his head stuck under the hood of a car, his usual position. I slammed the door of the old VW van. "Thanks for lunch." I waved off the guy I had hitched a ride with after our lunch date.

I adjusted my black wrap dress so it was wrapped in all the right places.

Contorting his body, Derek stood up and turned around. He took the dirty oily rag from the back pocket of his blue mechanic overalls and wiped his hands, leaving some smudging on them. He pushed the large-frame black glasses up on the bridge of his nose.

It was a shame he covered up that body; I bet every single woman in Walnut Grove, Kentucky would take their car to him for all of their repairs if he wore a white v-neck t-shirt and a pair of snug Wranglers. Most of the time women got lost in his steel-blue eyes, so bright against his black hair. But if they only knew what was underneath all the clothes…

For years Derek and I used to go skinny dipping in the river until one day our stares lingered a little too long, and we realized our bodies where no longer those of little kids. Derek had grown into a hot dude right before my eyes and I never saw it coming. Too bad I could only think of him like a brother.

“I need your help.” I stuck my hands out to the side like I was on a balance beam, trying to keep my five-foot-eight frame upright on my high-heels because the loose pieces of the beat-up concrete walkway made me a little wobbly. I grabbed the lanyard from around my neck with my Porty Morty’s ID stuck in the clear pouch and threw it in my bag. “I’m not going to need that any time soon. What about that help?”

I hopped onto a piece of concrete slab that was mostly intact, once again having to readjust the wrap dress.

“I learned my lesson a long time ago that before I agree to help you with anything that I better have all the details of what it is you want.” His brows frowned, his eyes narrowed. “Every single detail.”

“Simple. I need a car.” I took the toe of my heel and batted around a piece of loose concrete to avoid all of the questions that were going to follow.

"No way, no how am I going to help you out." Derek looked over my shoulder at the beat-up van. His five o'clock shadow was a little thicker than normal.

The gears grinded before the driver of the VW gave us the peace sign and took off.

I took a couple steps forward and rubbed the back of my hand down his chin.

"No wonder you can't get any ladies. Clean yourself up." I messed up his hair.

He jerked his head back. He quirked his eyebrow questioningly.

"Who was that?" He asked in a "good ole boy" voice and jerked his head to the right, getting a better view of the VW.

"Gary. . .um. . .Barry I think." I shrugged off his interrogation. "Lunch Date Dot Com."

"Good grief." Derek shook his head. "I'd rather stay single."

Lunch Date Dot Com was a dating website where you met for lunch on your lunch breaks. I didn't even bother to read the guy's profile before I accepted his lunch offer because I was starving and I needed a ride to come out here and see Derek.

"So what about that car?" I wiggled my brows that were in desperate need of a wax.

Given my current money status, I was going to have to settle for Trixie's hot pink jeweled tweezers she picked up on her weekly run to the Dollar Store.

"I don't think so." Derek resumed his position under the hood of the elevated car. "Besides, where is your company car from Porty Morty's?"

"I got fired," I murmured. I adjusted the tight black Diane Von Furstenberg dress I had picked up from the local Salvation Army. Wrapping a piece of my shoulder-length honey-colored hair behind my ear, I batted my grey eyes and used fifteen hundred dollars cash to fan my face. "I've got fifteen hundred dollars. You can use it to fix that little concrete problem you have." I pointed to the chipped-up material.

"Laurel London, did you say fired?" Derek swiftly turned back around and waved a wrench in the air until he saw the cash. There was a little twinkle in his eye. I knew Derek like the back of my hand. He loved cash just as much as I did.

I waved the dough under his nose. "That is why I need a new car."

When I heard a faint sniff as the cash passed his left nostril, I knew he was on the line. It was time for me to hook him and reel him in.

"Trixie will skin my hide if I take that stolen cash."

"Stolen?" Okay. I was officially offended. "You think I stole this money? I want you to know," I jerked my shoulders back and cocked my chin in the air. His eyes were on the cash. "This is guilt money from Morty. That no good sonofa…," I muttered a few curse words under my breath.

"See, why do you have to go around talking like that?" Derek asked. His face contorted. "That along with your…um…sticky fingers don't make me want to do any sort of favors for you anymore."

"Sticky fingers? Geesh." I threw my hands in the air. "When is this town ever going to get over that?"

"Over it?" He laughed. "Over it?"

"Yeah, heard you the first time." I spoke softly and narrowed my eyes.

"You have pick-pocketed every single person in the town, not to mention how you hacked into the Wilsons' accounts after they took you in."

"Oh that. Phish!" I gestured. "That was seven years ago. I was fifteen years old. Besides, it wasn't like you weren't right there with me." I tapped my temple and then brushed a strand of my hair behind my ear and again fanned myself with the money. Clearly the sticky, humid weather wasn't doing me any favors. "I clearly remember you threading the fishing line on the Quantum Rod and Reel you had on your Christmas list. I played Santa, that's all." I shrugged, recalling all the crappy Christmas presents the orphanage gave all of us year after year and when I had decided to use the Wilsons' credit card to buy all the orphans real Christmas presents.

"It was your chance to get out of the big house and you blew it." Derek shook his head. He put the wrench in his back pocket and crossed his arms in front of him. "Anyone would have given their arm to get out of there and have a real Christmas for once."

True, true. I didn't have a leg to stand on with his argument.

I admired Derek. He got out of the orphanage with a great job and was working on his dream to become a police officer. He was almost finished with night classes at the University of Louisville.

"You didn't tell me the truth about those Christmas presents or I would've never shown up to meet you." Derek's lip turned up in an Elvis kind of way exposing a small portion of his pearly white teeth and deepening the dimple on his cheek. A distant twinkle flickered in his blue eyes. "You sure were believable when you told me they bought all the presents for the orphanage. Genius in fact." He pointed his finger at me. "I credit you for me wanting to be a cop. Since I know how you work, I'm going to be able to figure out how criminal minds work."

"Ha, ha." I slowly clapped my hands. "Very funny," I sneered.

"That was then." I waved the money again. "Before I made myself an honest girl and got a big girl job."

"Getting fired from Porty Morty's is a big girl job?" Derek chuckled. "How did you get fired from selling port-a-lets?"

I wasn't sure, but I detected a little hint of sarcasm in his tone.

"Morty let me go. Something about overhead and people aren't using port-a-potties anymore." My mouth dipped down.

"Where are the people pooping?" Derek's nose curled up.

"Got me." I shrugged. "Anyway, I need a set of wheels. That old 1977 beat-up Caddy was Morty's. He let me borrow it because my job was to get all of those outdoor venues to use Porty Morty's at their events. He made me give it back. I need a new set of wheels to find a job before Trixie finds out. She is going to kill me when I tell her Morty let me go."

Kill might be a strong word to use, but she wasn't going to be happy. Trixie had been in charge of the orphanage for years. It just so happened that when I turned eighteen, the state shut down the orphanage forcing Trixie to retire.

She said I needed guidance and in no formal sort of way she became my guardian. The only mother figure I'd known. In truth, I think she was really worried about me and wanted to make sure I did well. She was the first person to ever see potential in me. Then and there I'd decided I was going to make something of myself. She got me the job with Morty and I'd been working there ever since, bringing home a steady paycheck. Not much. But it was reliable. I was able to get a studio apartment, though my rent was always a tad bit late.

"I love you like a sis' and all, but how am I going to do that?"

"You got all those cars out there." I pointed to the field filled with abandoned cars that Derek used for parts. The grass had grown up around the tires which were probably dry-rotted, and they all had a little rust. Nothing a set of new tires and paint job couldn't fix.

"Those old clunkers? Nah, I don't have anything that's reliable and good enough to drive." He bit the side of his lip.

I waved the money again. "Morty called it compensation." Compensation my ass. It was guilt money. "It's all I have to get me a car. Come on. I've been on the straight and narrow for five years. You know it, and I know it. All I need is a car to get around so I can get another job."

Jobs were slim pickings in our little town of twelve hundred. Louisville was only thirty minutes away and surely I could score some sort of job there.

"I don't know." Derek shook his head. "There really isn't anything out there that fifteen hundred will fix."

I put my hand up to my brows to cover the sun beaming down and scanned the field. There had to be something.

"What about that one?" I pointed to the black-and-white-colored one to the far right. Sort of off by itself.

"That old '62 Plymouth Belvedere?" Derek laughed so hard, he was hyperventilating.

"Yeah. What's wrong with it?" There was no humor in my voice. "Other than the faded sign on the side."

"Come on." He tugged his head to the side. "The engine may need a good clean up."

"Okay." Like I knew what that meant. I followed him to the edge of the grass and stopped to take my shoes off. The heels would've gotten stuck in the ground and I had to keep them clean. It was going to be a long time before I bought any new shoes. "Oh." My face contorted. Up close I could tell the old Belvedere had seen better days.

I swiped my hand across the dusty old door.

"Taxi?" I laughed, never recalling a taxi service in Walnut Grove.

"I got that when the police academy tore down the old building on the edge of town." He pointed to me. Derek was also training to be a deputy with the sheriff's department. On Monday and Wednesday he drove to the University of Louisville for the police academy. "Remember? I told you about how they had us running around the old building and things popped out at us and we had to assess the situation before we pulled the trigger."

Vaguely I remember him saying something about it.

"Still. I'm serious, Derek. I need a ride." I tapped the car. "Even if it does say taxi."

"Can you imagine if you drove that thing down Main Street." He slapped his knee. "Everyone would know you were crazy, not just wonder."

"We could repaint it," I suggested.

"We? We?" He gestured between the two of us. "You mean me."

"Come on," I begged. "You are my only hope of not letting Trixie down. You don't want to do that, do you? After she has done for us. This place." I pointed to his garage.

Trixie owned the property and when Derek graduated from mechanic school, she gave him the run-down building that he had turned into his business.

"Oh." He shook his finger at me. "You are good at playing the guilt card. I worked hard for this place. I went to work every morning before school and every day after school."

"Yeah, but Trixie gave you the car to do it." I reminded him of her other good deed.

His chest heaved up and down as he let out a heavy sigh. He knew I had him.

"The only real problem with it is the rust." He rubbed his hands along the side of the car and walked back to the bumper. "It was garage kept and it has low mileage. I probably should have covered it with a tarp or something, but I thought I'd be using it for parts. I suppose it would look fine if you painted it."

"You can do that for me right?" I squinted to keep the sun out of my eyes. The skies were blue and the sun was bright.

"No. I don't do paint," he protested.

"I bet you could." I tilted my head around the edge of the car to see the other side.

"Laurel, you exhaust me." He bit the side of his lip.

I could tell he was thinking about it so I put the unexplained shadow behind me and batted my lashes. I put my hands together in a little praying way and mouthed please.

"Fine." He jammed his hands in the pockets of his overalls. "It's not going to be perfect," he warned.

"I don't care." I smiled from ear to ear. I held the money out in front of me.

"Nope. I'm not taking the only money you have." He shoved my hand back toward me. "Consider it an early Christmas gift."

"You do love me." I jumped up and down before throwing my arms around his neck.

"No. I love that Quantum Rod and Reel still." He gave me a slight hug back.

## Chapter Two

"Now what are we going to do?" I asked Henrietta as I held the refrigerator door wide open, hoping to find something, anything deep within the depths of the beat-up, dented box. Suddenly I wished I had taken the leftovers from Lunch Date Dot Com guy.

Meow. Henrietta, my cat, sat at my feet looking into the refrigerator.

Meow. She looked up at me and licked her lips.

"I promise I will find us something." I sighed. "Have I ever let you down?"

One night when Derek and I were teenagers hanging out at the river down at the docks doing what teenagers did (drinking) and we found Henrietta under a bush on the banks. Of course I took her home and didn't tell Trixie.

Henrietta wasn't a very quiet kitten and that night she cried and cried. I was too drunk to even hear her, but Trixie's super-sonic ears heard. Henrietta got me and her into trouble that night. Luckily Trixie let me keep her.

Henrietta pounced into the air, bringing me back to the present situation. She batted something between her front paws, a six-legged creature scurried out from under her.

Still hungry, I watched Henrietta pounce again because I knew the outcome of the play fight Henrietta thought she was doing with the insect. The insect knew it too. Dinner.

"Enjoy," I said and turned my attention back to the refrigerator.

My stomach growled. The dried-up slice of lemon wasn't going to cut it.

Henrietta licked her paws before running them across her ears. Satisfied with her snack, she looked back up at me.

I closed the fridge as the laptop dinged.

"Oh, live one." I rushed over to the futon and grabbed my laptop off the side table. "Let's see who is going to take me to lunch tomorrow."

Right or wrong, I never turned my laptop off. The dating website tab was open and I had a new message from Bob.

"Hi Bob." I scrolled down the screen to get a look at him. "Not bad."

I usually didn't go for the muscle types, especially the ones who wore wife-beater tees. Though I did have to admit, his handsome, good looks along with the pearly white smile did overcome the bulging pecs.

Meow. Henrietta had an opinion.

"Yeah. I think we might get a good juicy piece of salmon out of this one." I quickly typed a note back to Bob.

Bing.

"And Bob answered." I hit the open button of the message. He was unable to make a lunch date because of work, but he was more than happy to have dinner.

Hmm…dinner was a big commitment that I wasn't sure I was willing to do only because I would feel like I needed to keep the night going. Lunch was way better because we had to get back to work. At least I used to have to get back to work. I decided cocktails would be better and then it could extend to dinner if it went well. I dashed off a reply to Bob and looked at Henrietta.

"Let's go." I grabbed her hot pink, crystal-studded leash and clipped it on her collar.

She had gotten used to being on a leash when we lived at the children's home. The orphanage was in the country. We didn't have the extra money to buy a leash and Trixie made it clear that Henrietta was my responsibility. Derek and I had gone to Kmart to check out the cost of leashes and one stuck to my sticky fingers and fit Henrietta perfectly.

Trixie never asked where I had gotten it, nor did I tell her.

The efficiency I rented was on Second Street, a street over from The Cracked Egg. Henrietta and I definitely would score some food there. My best friend Gia Picerilli's family owned the greasy spoon, plus she worked there and knew my food situation.

I reached down and put my hand out. Henrietta brushed her back on my palm, stopping briefly to let me attach the leash. She loved going for walks.

At least it was sunny and warm, not raining like most spring days. Henrietta happily walked in front of me with her head high in the air. Sure we got strange looks from people who didn't know us and weren't use to seeing cats on leashes. Henrietta thought she was a dog. People who did know me, knew I was rarely without her.

We headed south on Second Street and left on Main. The street was already lined with parked cars. The Cracked Egg was known for its down-home country cooking. Some people traveled forty-five minutes just to get one of Mr. Chiconi's bacon, lettuce, and tomato sandwiches.

Just like always, all the café tables were taken, but not my stool at the left side of the bar.

Gia poured hot steaming coffee from the glass coffeepot and talked as fast as the liquid poured out.

"What are you doing here?" Gia asked over the crowd as she made her way down the counter. She looked back at the clock on the wall behind the counter. "Why aren't you at work?"

There was a puzzled look on her face. She pushed the pen behind her ear that was buried under her massive curly black hair that she had pulled into a low ponytail. Envy pinched me. I tucked a piece of my honey-colored, shoulder-length hair behind my ear and wished I had her full head of hair.

Gia always had that va-voom that guys loved. My va-voom was more like a torn off muffler. A little rough around the edges. I'm not saying I'm a dog, but Gia knew how to wear clothes, bright red lipstick and get a man. Me. . .not so much.

When anyone crossed me growing up, I'd take them down in a minute, never once thinking I was going to grow up one day and live among them. I was hell-bent on getting out of Walnut Grove when I turned eighteen. That didn't seem to happen.

"Well?" Gia kicked a small cage around the corner of the counter.

Henrietta knew the drill. The cage was for her and she knew when she got in, Gia gave her some leftover salmon or ham. Henrietta's favorite.

Gia leaned on her elbows and chomped on her gum only inches away from my face. The lines between her brows creased waiting for my answer.

"Morty Shelton fired me this morning." I flipped my cup over. I did air quotes. "Let me go."

My cheeks heated. I wondered how many people got fired from selling port-a-lets.

"Fired? Did you say fired? That can't be right. What is Morty thinking?" She shook her head like she was trying to see if it was working.

I nodded. "It's true." I sighed.

She poured the coffee in my cup and pushed the small bowl filled with creamer cups toward me. "He must not be thinking."

"Obviously he wasn't thinking." Anger boiled inside me. "I was the best salesperson he had. Not to mention the only salesperson he had."

Getting people to buy things to me came naturally. In fact, I had been selling things since I was eight years old. I would "collect" items from the foster families' houses.

All the other kids in the slammer, which was what we orphans called the orphanage, knew it too and would save the little bit of chore money we got and barter with me on the items I had "collected." A bar of Dove always went for a lot of money. Even the five-year-old orphans didn't want to use the cheap yellow bar with "soap" stamped on it. The smell alone made our bellies hurt.

"Carmine told me they got the big gig you have been working on. Without you that would have never happened." Gia walked back down the counter and filled empty mugs.

Carmine Picerilli, Gia's husband, was the only accountant in Walnut Grove. He rented out a little office in the top of the port-a-potty warehouse. Carmine did Porty Morty's accounting for free in exchange for free rent. Granted, you could almost lose your life climbing the tiny metal stairs to get to Carmine's office, but it had a great view once you were up there. His windows overlooked the entire river.

"Morty got the Underworld Music Festival account?" I asked a little louder than I probably should have. But I wanted to make sure she heard me over the crowd and clanking dishes.

Meow. Henrietta looked up at me from the little open door on the cage. Her pupils dilated.

The regular stool warmers, which were what we called the older men who came in every single morning to catch up with each other, swiveled their bodies toward me.

I grabbed my cup and took a sip to shut me up. I couldn't believe it. I had been working on the Underworld Music Festival account for a year.

Over a year ago I was at Food Town grocery shopping and picked up the Vogue Magazine at the checkout. That was the only time I got to read Vogue. Sometimes when I grabbed a cup of coffee at the Gas-N-Go, I'd linger at the counter and read the headlines of my favorite magazines—they were too darn expensive and so not in my budget—but the day I was in line at Food Town, I put back my milk and bought Vogue because there was an advertisement for the Underworld Music Festival.

They were having a contest where you could enter your city or town and the winner was where they would host the next festival. Walnut Grove, Kentucky, was perfect. We had plenty of farm land near the river. I knew it would be great for Walnut Grove's economy and a good client for Morty.

Visions of rows and rows of port-a-lets had danced in my head along with the dollar signs and a big bonus for me. Here we were today; the visions of dollar signs fallen and crumbled at my feet.

"Yes. Carmine said he was going to be busy the next few days trying to get all the permits needed for Morty." The bell over the diner door dinged. "Have a seat anywhere!" Gia hollered out to the people coming into the diner. She grabbed a couple of menus and followed them to their table.

My blood was boiling. Morty hadn't wanted to even consider the festival. When I told him about my idea for the festival, he said the family functions, the boat dock parties, funerals, and the Friendship Baptist Church revival was plenty to have on the calendar. I knew better. The economy wasn't growing. There was chatter that eventually Walnut

Grove would just merge with Louisville and become a suburb.

Ugh.

I didn't want that to happen. So I took matters into my own hands. In fact, I had to save up my own money to hop on the Greyhound Bus to New York and meet with the big publicity firm in charge of the festival. Little did I know that you had to have an appointment to be seen. The big doorman wasn't about to let me in.

I scribbled my name, number, and why I was there on a used gum wrapper I had found balled up in the bottom of my purse and left it with the doorman. I hadn't heard back so I guessed the doorman hadn't given my "note" to the publicity firm.

Gia came back and grabbed a fresh pot of coffee off the pot stand.

"Carmine said that all the plans will be completed in a couple of weeks. I told him that you told me you were turned away at the door." Gia talked fast.

The diner was getting busier by the minute.

"Some fancy woman with her black hair coiled into a bun on top of her head with chopsticks in it came to see Morty," Gia snorted. "Can you imagine putting chopsticks in your hair? Did you see anything like that when you went to New York?"

"There were a lot of things I had seen in New York that I wished I hadn't," I murmured trying to take in everything Gia was telling me—getting more and more pissed with each passing breath. "There is no way they will be able to set up a festival as big as Underworld in three weeks."

"The festival isn't in three weeks. The planning stage should be over in three weeks. Gee, Laurel, I'm so sorry. I know how much you worked on that account." Her perfectly lined red lips frowned.

"A year," my voice cracked. I bit my lip trying to hold back the urge to punch the counter. "Over a year."

In my spare time I had already put together a business plan that consisted of all the bands, their contact information and a preliminary schedule of events. I had even gone as far as contacting some of the big headliners and their agents in case I did hear back from the Underworld peeps.

All that work for nothing. If I could kill Morty Shelton and get away with it. . .I would. I glared. This whole idea of trying to get on the up and up was starting to have a stink to it.

"Damn Morty. He wants all the money and glory for himself. I landed that account." The more I thought about it, the more pissed off I got.

"What you are going to do for work now?" There was concern in her voice. Her eyes deepened.

"I was going to look through the help wanted ads in the Louisville Courier and see if there was a sales job." I made myself a mental note to go by the Walnut Grove Journal and see if there were any posted jobs.

"Sales?" Gia laughed.

"What?" I asked. "I did sales for Porty Morty's. Okay," I admitted. "Calling my job at Porty Morty's a sales position might be stretching it a bit but I did have to talk people into using port-a-lets at their functions."

"Do I need to remind you about your past sales history?" Gia asked bringing up my ever-so-stained past.

Once I was sent to a young couple that had just adopted a baby from overseas and felt guilty when all their family said there were plenty of orphans in the United States. Lucky me…they decided they would try their hand at fostering. Unfortunately the husband was an undercover cop. I didn't know about those Nanny cams, so when the good old cop and his wife played back the tapes and saw me having a vested interest in multiple items in their home, he had me arrested. Luckily, Trixie got me off…yet again. But that was a long time ago.

"You can always work here."

I lowered my eyes and curled my nose.

"Yes. I remember, but you have grown up." She smiled one of those sympathy smiles.

Let's just say that I was not very good at hearing complaints about Mr. Chiconi's food when I filled in for Gia when she had her wisdom teeth removed. Needless to say…I was never asked to fill in again.

"I'm sorry, Laurel. I know you had been working so hard on that account." Gia took in a deep breath before she let out a long sigh. Another group of people came into the diner and took the big six-top table in the front.

"How about an afternoon cocktail waitress over at Benny's?" I suggested because I needed a vodka.

"Laurel, that's not funny." She didn't find my humor endearing.

I'm glad she didn't because if she said yes, sadly I would've been walking to Benny's.

"Gia, it's going to be fine. I'm always fine." I was lying through my teeth. That no good Morty.

I'd love to get Morty in one of his port-a-lets and knock it over. I couldn't help but smile at images of crap rolling down Morty's bald head.

## Chapter Three

The next day was turning out much like the day before. Get up. Watch Henrietta hunt for a bug to eat. Look in the refrigerator at the dried lemon slice.

"Not today." I slammed the refrigerator door shut when I realized I had let the refrigerator go a few days without food in it.

Mrow. Henrietta let out a little cry of hope that I had found a morsel of food. She looked at me with her big star-shaped eyes.

"It won't be long until I get a job," I assured her like she knew exactly what I was saying. "I can feel it in my bones."

Truth be told, the only thing I could feel in my bones was hunger.

"Either way," I bent down to rub her, "I will walk to the Dollar Store if I have to and grab a couple of Parts of Meat."

She darted underneath the futon like she knew what Parts of Meat was. Every time I had to pinch a few pennies, I would pick up a couple of cheapo cans of Parts of Meat cat food. Henrietta wouldn't even look at her plate when she saw it.

"Snob." I glanced at the futon. Henrietta's long grey tail swept across the floor a few times.

I unhooked my phone from the charger and threw it in my hobo. Enough was enough. It was time I stopped moping. It was also past time to stop hoping that Morty was going to call me back new that the Underworld Music Festival people were in town. It wasn't going to happen, and I had to get my butt in gear.

I darted out of the efficiency and down the metal stairs. If I walked north on Second Street and took a right on River Road, the Walnut Grove Journal was down a little ways on the left. It was located right next to Porty Morty's.

It was as good a time as any to go in and see Anita Musgrave, the editor, journalist, photographer, and only employee of the paper. She'd been there as long as I could remember. Our last meeting hadn't been all that great; she was the one who I had given my essay to that fateful Christmas I had spent with Pastor Wilson.

Anita who ooh'ed and ahh'ed over how great the Wilsons were for not only taking me in but also buying all the Christmas gifts for the orphans.

She'd called the local news station that just had to do a feel-good story on the good Pastor and Rita. Through gritted teeth, the Pastor smiled for the camera and did an on-spot interview claiming it was God's divine whisper that told them to give all of those nice, expensive presents to the orphans because the orphans were God's children too, just like every other boy and girl who had a family home.

Needless to say, to this day all the participants in the situation ran in the opposite direction when they see me. That included Anita Musgrave.

When I entered the building, I found Anita sitting behind the big metal desk with papers scattered all over the top. More littered the floor around her feet.

She gave me the briefest of glances before she returned to her work.

"I don't have time for fooling around." Her head was bent in concentration. "What do you want now?"

I took out enough change from my hobo to pay for a paper. "I would like a copy of your latest paper."

I waited for her to respond.

The years hadn't been so good to Anita. Her waist had thickened; her face was heavier. And she had a five o'clock shadow on her upper lip.

"Have you ever thought about making an appointment with Kim at Shear Illusions?" I ran my hands over my own thick eyebrows in need of a little grooming.

"Are you telling me you hate my hair?" She looked up, shooting me a death stare.

"Not at all. Just asking." I looked away.

Anita was in no mood for me to give her beauty advice. Nor did it look like she was in the mood to clean up the messy joint.

"I just threw yesterday's papers in the dumpster outside." She pointed to the one on the side of Porty Morty's. "You can get one from there."

"Fine." I huffed and pushed the door back open.

I slipped across to the other side of the dock to where the dumpster was and put my change back in my bag. I slid the little door on the side of the dumpster. The papers were there and so was Morty's half-eaten breakfast sandwich.

I knew it was his because it's what he had every day and it made him very gassy. White egg omelet with green peppers. I tried to tell him to lay off the peppers, but he never listened. He stunk the place up worse than the used port-a-lets we got back from clients.

The buzz of a speedboat grew closer. There weren't many boats zipping on the river this early in the morning. I scanned each direction to see whcre it was coming from. Suddenly the speedboat rounded the corner, gliding through the turn.

The closer the boat got to Porty Morty's dock, the slower it went. The driver stood up as he steered and his hand covered his eyes as he scanned the land as he pulled his fancy shmancy boat up to Morty's dock.

"That's not a…," I stopped myself from yelling after I realized the roar of the fast boat's engine was way louder than my voice. "A dock for gas," I muttered.

Boaters were always stopping at Porty Morty's to see if there was gas or a little snack store on the dock. For years I told Morty he should invest in some sort of little gas station, but that was another good idea he refused to use.

The boat driver was dressed in a white button down, white pants, and white shiny shoes. His gold watch caught the sun just right and the flash blinded me.

The sun was shining and the air was warm. I took advantage of the benches and the beautiful view of the river and sat down.

I opened the paper and thumbed right past The Hub section and to the help wanted section.

Originally, The Hub section was supposed to be about events around Walnut Grove, but turned into gossip central from an anonymous contributor. Trixie loved to keep me up to date on what was happening. So I resisted the urge, which reminded me that I had better stop by her house and let her know I had been fired before my news made The Hub section of the Walnut Grove Journal.

My eyes darted around wondering if I was going to be next week's gossip.

I swung my feet back and forth, accidentally hitting a walnut that was under there. I watched it roll and then slid my eyes to the guy that had gotten out of the boat to tie up.

"Seriously, Morty should put up a sign that says the dock isn't a gas station," I said to myself and watched asshole Morty walk down the dock. "Fall in, bastard," I said hoping Morty would make a misstep right into the river.

My cell rang. I pulled it out of my bag and saw that the number on the screen of my super cheap flip phone was Derek.

"The car is painted and ready. I'm driving it over," he said. "Where are you? Home?"

"No." I was too distracted by Morty and boat guy to listen.

"Okay. I'll head to Trixie's," Derek said.

"No!" I shouted into the phone. "I haven't told Trixie about losing my job. I need to be the one to tell her. I'm down on the dock's right by Porty Morty's."

The driver of the boat glanced my way. I let my hair fall down into my face to give me a little more privacy.

"What in the hell have you been doing with yourself the past couple of days?"

"Taking it easy," I said. "Lying low. Real low."

The sound of two men arguing made me look up. Morty and the boat guy were having a heated conversation on the dock. I made a slight part in my hair and snuck a peek at their body language. Morty's bald head was shining like a diamond in the bright sun.

"Hey, have you passed the Dollar Store yet?" I asked knowing he was going to have to drive right past it.

"Getting ready to. Why? Trixie need some powder?" he asked.

"No. Henrietta needs a can of food."

"Fine. I'll stop," he added.

"Two?" I asked hastily.

"See you in a minute." I could tell from his tone that I was pushing my limit.

We hung up just in time for me to see that the boater and Morty's argument was escalating. The man was jabbing his finger in Morty's chest. The sunshine pinged off his big gold ring and the sunspot hit me straight in the eye.

The guy stepped one foot out of the boat and kept the other foot in. He lifted out two Styrofoam coolers, kind of like the ones Morty used to store the blue sanitizer pellets for the port-a-lets that we took to events. The smell-good kind—great for disguising the poop smell.

Morty's five-foot frame stood firm, holding his ground. He was not in his usual sweat suit attire. He was actually dressed in a nice suit I was sure had come from K-Mart since it was the only store in Walnut Grove that sold clothes of any kind. Morty never left Walnut Grove. Not even for clothes.

The man was already back in the speed boat and turned the motor over, giving it a little vroom. Morty greeted Pastor Wilson who was at the top of the gang plank of the dock and craning his neck to get a look at the boat. He and Morty shook hands as Morty grabbed Pastor Wilson by the elbow and jerked him around toward the building like he didn't want the pastor looking at the boat.

Morty picked up one of the coolers and stuck it in Pastor Wilson's arms. After talking the two of them disappeared into the old building.

The roaring sound of the speed boat caught my attention, though I found it strange that Pastor Wilson had paid Morty a visit. The revival wasn't until the fall and that was months away. In the years I had worked there, Pastor Wilson never came by. Morty always went to him for the revival details since the pastor avoided me at all costs.

"Good 2 Go," I read the name on the stern of the boat just before it rounded the corner from where it had come.

Beep, beep.

I jumped around. A big yellow car had pulled up and parked behind the bench. Derek jumped out.

"Here." He threw the keys toward me and held out his other hand where the yellow bag from the Dollar Store dangled from his grip.

"What is that?" I squinted and realized it was the rusty old black-and-white Belvedere that was now a rusty old yellow Belvedere. "I mean…" I swallowed hard. "You couldn't cover up the taxi sign?" I pointed to the door and thanked my lucky stars he had given me the old cab.

"The sign kept bleeding through." He seemed disappointed by my hesitation. "What did you expect for free, Laurel?"

True. He did have a point. I had to keep reminding myself this set of wheels was only temporary. Only temporary.

"It's great. It really is." I wiggled my brows.

Trying to be cool, I threw the keys up in the air. They slipped through my fingers and landed on the ground. Epic fail. I reached down and grabbed them. Derek didn't seem amused.

"And it's going to help me get a job!" Damn Morty. I glanced toward the worn-down warehouse.

"Where are you going to apply first?" Derek did his best football punt on the stray walnut on the ground. Walnuts were everywhere, hence the name Walnut Grove.

"I was thinking about going to Quick Copy." I took the paper from under my armpit. "They are hiring sales reps."

For the first time, I felt my nerves bubbling up. I never had my own car and I never had to actually go find a job.

I gripped the keys tighter. “This is mine, right?” I had to clarify he was giving me the car and not taking my fifteen hundred dollars as a down payment on a lease.

“Yes. The title is in the glove box. Thanks for taking the junker off my hands.” Derek smiled. “So you know how to sell copiers, service copiers and all the products?”

What? Of course I didn’t. But what was this? An interrogation?

“Do you doubt my abilities after all these years?” I jabbed him in the bicep. “I can learn anything. Besides annual bonuses, there is even a car that goes with the job.”

“You have a car.” We both looked back at the big yellow rusty hunk. “The world is your oyster.”

“One problem.”

“What’s that?”

“I don’t like oysters.”

## Chapter Four

"Fill 'er up!" I yelled to Clyde Yap out the Belvedere window—once I figured out how to roll them down—when I pulled up to the gas pumps at the Gas-N-Go.

There weren't a lot of bells and whistles to the Old Girl, that was what I had named her, the Old Girl. She was worth every single penny I paid. Free.

The Gas-N-Go was the only filling station in town that filled your tank and cleaned your windshield.

"Laurel London?" Clyde thrust his head into the driver's side window. A little too far, causing me to nearly jump out of my skin. "Where did you get this car?"

His highly starched shirt barely moved when he planted his elbows on the window frame waiting for my answer to his question. His beady eyes gave me the stare down.

"I—" I was interrupted by Baxter Thacker, owner of Gas-N-Go, when he cleared his throat.

He stood in the doorway of the gas station, his arms crossed over his large barreled chest. His eyes beat down on me. Baxter was not one I would want to meet in a dark alley at night. He was also one I never tried to cross when I was growing up at the orphanage. He made it very clear when Derek worked there that I was to come nowhere near the joint. Besides, the headless bald eagle tattoo on his forearm always gave me the creeps. He was a bad ass to the bone. No one crossed Baxter Thacker. Not even me.

"You better get on out of here before Baxter pulls out a gun or something." Clyde tapped the top of my hood. Clyde had been working for Baxter for as long as I could remember. He and Trixie were friends. We used Clyde's Moose membership to get into the Moose lodge sometimes.

"I'm a paying customer. I have the right to be here!" My voice escalated as I looked over at Baxter. His eyes narrowed. "I need gas." I plucked a twenty out of my purse that was sitting on the passenger seat and dangled it up in the air so Baxter could get a good look.

I should've only gotten ten dollars of gas and left the twenty to get some groceries. But I was probably going to need all twenty dollars worth since I was going to have to drive to Louisville and submit some applications if the Quick Copy idea didn't pan out.

Louisville was the closest "big" city to Walnut Grove and most Walnut Grove citizens worked in Louisville.

Property taxes were much cheaper here and the drive was only twenty minutes, thirty if you got behind a tractor.

Cough, Cough. Baxter did some sort of pretend cough to get my attention, his feet firmly on the ground, body now square and arms to his sides.

He let out another sound. I wasn't sure if it was a grunt or a burp, either way, he turned around and went back into the station to do whatever it was that Baxter did.

"Fine." Clyde took the money with his dirty hands, black underneath his nails, and took the nozzle off the pump before trying to figure out where the gas tank was.

"You want to tell me what you are up to?" he asked. The baseball cap was a good cover up for his balding head. He picked at the dirt around the base of his nails. "Or am I going to have to hear all about this from Trixie?"

Clyde had taken a fondness to Trixie. But in true Trixie fashion, she claimed she never did want nor need a man, though she spent a lot of time with Clyde. I was sure she had a little tender spot in her heart for him although she'd never admit it.

Countless times when Clyde would visit the orphanage for what Trixie called "meetings," she would put a note on the office door. We knew exactly what their "meeting" was about when we heard grunting coming from behind the office door.

"Morty has the old car in the shop," I lied and picked at the torn leather on the seat between my legs. In the rearview mirror I noticed Pepper Spivy walking on the sidewalk away from her parked car. When she noticed it was me in the car, she rushed to the other side of the street. "Derek gave me this old thing."

There was no way, no how I was going to tell Clyde that I had been fired. He'd tell Trixie. And if I told him before I told Trixie, she'd be in an uproar. It was best to keep my tale from everyone until I did find a job.

"What's it with her?" I pointed over to Pepper.

She stood across the street in her black pin-striped pant suit, her dishwater brown hair neatly cut into a bob that hit a tiny bit below her cheek line. She waved something in the air.

"Hold on." Clyde held up his finger before he ran across the street, almost getting hit by an oncoming car. He and Pepper exchanged a few words between a couple glances my way before he ran back over.

I gave her a little spirit finger wave, but she turned her nose up at me.

"What's that?" I poked my head out of the window to see if I could get a look at the paper Pepper had given him.

"Walnut Grove Savings Bank is hiring for a new teller and Baxter told her she could post a flyer in the window. When she saw you, she wanted to stay as far away as possible." Clyde tapped the nozzle on the edge of the gas tank before he stuck it back in the pump.

"Seriously?" My mouth dropped. I craned my neck to see if I could give Pepper a death stare, but she was already walking back to her car. "People in this town need to realize I have grown up."

I give Pepper the death stare when her car zoomed by. She gave me the bird. I would make sure to sit at her table when I went to The Cracked Egg. Sometimes she worked there as a fill-in when Gia's dad needed her, and it was good side money for her.

"It's hard to ask the good citizens of Walnut Grove to forget how you terrorized the community for years. After all Pepper did give you a cleaning job at the bank and you took advantage of her and the city by using all those debit cards from the bank customers to charge over five hundred dollars worth of pizzas to be delivered to the orphanage." Clyde grabbed the squeegee and flung it to the ground getting all the excess fluid off before he ran it across the Belvedere's windshield.

"Good gravy. It. Was. Pizza. Have you ever eaten fried bologna seven days in a row?

"I can't say I have," he shook his head.

"Well, we orphans did and pizza sounded good." I rolled my eyes and turned the ignition on. "When is this po-dunk town ever going to give me a second chance?"

"Unfortunately they've given you multiple chances. More chances than a cat gets in lives." He slammed the squeegee in the dirty bucket of windshield wiper fluid sitting next to the pump.

The Gas-N-Go bell dinged when another car pulled up on the other side of the pump. He put both hands on my window sill.

He leaned in and whispered, "I don't know what is going on with you, but you better make good by Trixie. She's done a lot for you, young lady."

"Don't you think I know that?" I asked.

"Hold on." Clyde rushed inside the gas station only to come right back out holding something up for me to see. He jabbed his hand in my window. "Here. Air freshener on the house."

"Thanks, Clyde!" I took the hot pink fuzzy dice of the package. It smelled just like fresh cotton linens. "That is so nice." I hung the dice from the rearview mirror.

"I believe in you." He smiled, tapping the car door.

With a full tank of gas, I threw the old Belvedere in drive. Even though I should go put in some applications, I wanted to see just how well the Old Girl could handle the back road curves of Walnut Grove.

# Chapter Five

Somehow I was going to show this town that I, Laurel London, was going to make something of myself and was going to do it on the up-and-up. Granted I did hack a few accounts to order pizzas or charged Christmas gifts on the good ole Pastor's credit card, but it was all done in the spirit of giving and with a good heart and good intentions. Well…the good intentions part might be a little bit of a stretch, but the good heart thing was all true.

Being an orphan was hard. Everyone always stared and pointed when they saw Trixie and the gang or even just a few of us walking to the Dollar Store or even the Gas-N-Go for a Slurpee, which was a real treat.

Their sad eyes would always drop in a way that made me feel ashamed. I didn't want anyone feeling sorry for me and that was probably why I set out to prove them wrong.

I was bound and determined to get out of Walnut Grove and find my path, but with no money, I had no other place to go. My grades in school didn't offer me the skills I needed to go to college or get a big paying job and I'd needed Trixie's help to pull strings to get me the job at Porty Morty's.

Without realizing my speed and the curves on River Road, I got lost in thought and drummed my fingers on the steering wheel trying to come up with a way to prove to everyone that I had changed.

"Oh shit!" I swerved the Old Girl into the ditch, avoiding the deer that had jumped out in front of me.

My heart pounded a mile a minute. I threw the gear shift in park before I hopped out to see if I missed it or not. Deer could do serious damage to a car.

I rubbed the bumper of the car, happy to see there was no damage and I could just pull right back onto the road. I rubbed my forehead. I swore my mind was playing tricks on me.

"Where the hell you going?" someone asked through a cough that was so loud it would rattle windows. "You almost hit me!"

I turned toward the man who was definitely not a deer. His muscular arms were wedged into a black t-shirt. He pushed himself up from the ground. His five-foot-ten frame looked like it was built for action. Hurting someone kind of action. Not to mention he had on a pair of black leather gloves.

"Oh my God!" I rushed over to him hoping to beg for his forgiveness because if I didn't, it looked like he was going to do me in. "You aren't a deer? Are you okay?"

"Deer? Are you blind?" His hands could easily cover the top of a table. He swiped them down his jeans to get the dirt off of them.

"I'm so sorry. I was in deep thought." I put my hands out as I got closer to him. "It's been a bad day. Bad week," I murmured.

His dark eyes glared at me. There wasn't a hint of letting me off the hook anywhere on his stern face.

"You shouldn't be driving! I want to talk to your boss." He jabbed his finger toward the Old Girl.

"I…," I stammered. "Boss?"

He interrupted, "The least you can do is give me a ride to Louisville." He passed me, walking toward the car.

"That's like thirty minutes away. And that's on a good day if there aren't any tractors on the road, and then it could take like an hour."

If he thought I was driving him to Louisville he was crazy, though it would give me the motivation to get some of those applications out.

He stopped, his back to me. His upper body went up and down as he took a deep breath and released it. With his back still turned, he lifted up the back of his black t-shirt over the waistband of his dark jeans and exposed the butt of a gun.

"Do I need to say more?" He didn't wait for an answer; he just kept walking toward the car.

"Nope. No more." I bit my lip and looked around. Give them what they want, I repeated what I had heard on cop television shows over and over in my head.

I was about to be killed. I wasn't going to be able to show Walnut Grove how I was going to turn my life around. No one was going to show up at my funeral. I could hear them now, "She tried to con the wrong person this time. She deserved what she got."

"Do I need to show you my little friend again?" he asked, obviously trying to get me to hurry along.

His question hung in the distance between us, unmasked, unanswered. He got into the back seat of the Old Girl and shut the door.

My legs didn't want to move. No matter how much I tried. I was paralyzed in fear.

The thought of bolting off into the woods crossed my mind, but I knew the river was just on the other side. I could jump in and swim toward town, but knew the man's gun was a lot faster than I could dog paddle.

He had rolled down the window and stuck his head out. He tapped his fancy big gold watch on his wrist with a gloved finger. "I don't have all day." With his other hand, he waved his gun in the air.

Lickety split I rushed back to the car and got in.

"Airport Hotel." He rolled the window back up and laid his friend on the seat next to him. He patted the gun. "Just to make sure you don't do any funny business."

I gulped. "You know what?" I asked and turned around in my seat. "I don't know who you are or what you want with me, but I am not comfortable with that pointing directly at me. So you need to put it away right now."

He looked up, our eyes met for the first time. His lips drew into a tight smile. "You are feisty. I think we are going to get along just fine." He took the gun off the seat and put it back into his waistband.

I watched to make sure the gun was out of sight. He took a wad of cash out of his pocket and reached over the front seat. My eyes danced with excitement. There were a lot of things I could do with that money.

"This should cover the cost of the taxi fee and your memory loss of ever seeing me." His voice threatened. He let the money fall on the seat next to me.

There were at least six hundred-dollar bills lying there.

"Airport Hotel." I clicked my tongue before I threw the gear shift in drive and slowly pulled out of the ditch heading back toward the airport. "You staying long? What were you doing in the woods?"

"You ask a lot of questions for a taxi cab driver." He crossed his massive arms across his chest. "I'm mainly paying you for memory loss. Got it?"

I glanced back in the rearview, he was staring out the window. There was a deep scar from his temple to his ear lobe and he had his arm propped up on the door with his hand dangling down, the other clasped it.

"Taxi cab driver?" I slanted him the question before it dawned on me that he thought that because the Old Girl's door had a faded taxi sign on it. The money. I needed the money. "Yes. I do like to pass the time with my passengers."

If he thought I was a taxi and it meant I was going to let him out without getting killed and have a few hundred dollars in my pocket, I could lie like a rug.

"Airport Hotel. Next stop." I squinted as I pulled back out on River Road, in fear a lightning bolt was going to come down from the heavens and strike me because at some point all of my recent lies were going to catch up to me.

His hard jaw tensed. His sharp, squinty eyes stared back at me in the rearview. He meant business. "Tell me about this little town of yours."

Obviously it was okay for him to ask questions about me, but I couldn't ask questions about him. I rubbed the back of my neck. Suddenly it felt tense. In the back of my hypochondriac mind, I couldn't help but think about my family health history.

I could have some sort of crazy disease and not even know it. Lately, that was one thing I had been battling with. Where I came from. Over and over Trixie told me I didn't come with papers, but there has to be a history somewhere.

What if I needed a kidney or something? My stomach hurt just thinking about it.

“I said,” the guy yelped, “tell me about your town.

“There isn’t much to tell.” I stalled trying to keep my cool. I tried to keep my teeth from chattering.

Neck hurting, chattering teeth. Was I nervous or was I getting the first symptoms of some disease?

“Isn’t there an orphanage here?” he asked, getting my attention again.

“Yeah.” I snickered. “It’s closed down now.”

“Really? Where did they put the kids?” he asked.

“We grew up.” I shrugged and made idle chit-chat so I could quickly pass the time and get him and that firearm out of my life.

“We?” he questioned. I could feel his foot tapping the floor behind my seat in sort of a nervous way. “You lived there?”

“Yeah.”

“Man, I bet that was a bitch,” he said with disgust.

“The orphanage wasn’t, but the foster families were. Gee.” The Old Girl was flying around the curves. “A whole ’nother story.”

“Slow down!” He gripped the handle on the door.

"Sorry," I murmured. "I guess you brought up some buried memories. How did you hear about the orphanage?"

"A friend of a friend grew up there."

"Oh, who?" I asked.

"I'm sure you wouldn't know him."

"Try me." I dared him. "I was there from birth to eighteen. I bet I know him or heard of him."

I looked back in the mirror at him. He glared at me. His brows drew together in an angry frown.

"You don't," he asserted. His lip cocked up to one side. His nostrils flared.

I dropped the subject. It was apparent he was becoming agitated with me and I didn't want that to happen.

He looked out the window. I took the opportunity to slip my phone out of my pocket and predial 911.

"Don't even think about using it," he warned and stuck his leather-gloved hand over the seat, gesturing for the phone.

"I wasn't going to use it." I put it over my shoulder and slapped it in his glove.

"That is why it has 911 typed on the screen?" He rolled down the window and threw the phone out.

"Hey! That was my phone!" I screamed.

"I gave you plenty of cash to get a new one. Besides," he snarled, "that one was way out of date."

True. It was Trixie's old flip phone. Morty wasn't paying me enough to afford a new one and a place of my own. The plan I was on was so cheap that I was sure they didn't have phone plans like that with fancy phones.

"Here." He threw a couple more hundreds over the seat. "That should be plenty for one of those fancy phones. Say, where is your taxi meter?"

"Umm." Shit! I didn't think about the taxi meter thing. Think, think. I knew I had to come up with a good story or he was going to off me right then and there. "It was in my phone that you threw out the window on…on an app."

"That old thing had the ability to put apps on it?" he questioned. His voice was low and smooth.

He wasn't buying into my lie.

Something told me there wasn't anyone that crossed him and I couldn't get him out of Walnut Grove fast enough. Though my sense of curiosity did make me wonder why he was in the country part of town.

I looked in the rearview mirror about to ask him why he was in Walnut Grove, but when our eyes met a sudden chill crept up my spine. I shifted my eyes forward, focusing on the lines on the road.

With my hands at two and ten on the wheel, I didn't say another word until we reached the Airport Hotel.

"Thanks so much," I quipped, throwing the gear shift into park.

I couldn't get him out of my fake cab fast enough.

"Now." The big guy leaned forward placing his arms across the back of the front seat with his chin resting on them. Hot air darted in my ear when he whispered, "You be back here tomorrow morning at nine a.m. Sharp. I will pay you double what I paid you today. No questions asked."

Before I could protest, he was out of the car adjusting his clothes. He wasn't fooling me. I knew he was rearranging his gun so it was out of sight.

He turned around and motioned for me to roll down the window. "Remember, you've never seen me."

"One question." I put my hands together in a begging, pleading way. "Are you going to hurt anyone in Walnut Grove?"

It was a legit question.

"You see, I'm not the most popular gal in town and I really want to get on the up-and-up," I started to tell him my tale. "And if I'm going to kind of turn my life around, I don't want to be known as the girl who helped you out. Whoever you are," I mumbled.

He stared at me and burst out laughing.

"No. I'm not going to hurt anyone as long as anyone stays out of my business and I get what I want." The laughter took a spiral downward as his lips tightened into a serious glare. "Tony. My name is Tony. See you tomorrow at nine a.m."

"Sharp."

"Yep, I think we are gonna get along just fine while I'm in town." Tony looked at me intently before he turned around. He strode through the door of the hotel, never once turning back.

# Chapter Six

"Walnut Grove." Someone opened the back passenger side, opposite where Tony had sat, throwing a duffle bag to the other side and slammed the door.

"Oh my God! You scared me!" My hands clasped over my heart. "Get out of my car!"

I jerked around, gripped the back of my seat, and glared at the hazel eyes staring back at me.

Okay, so he was hot. For a second, I wished I had looked at him before I told him to get out.

"You aren't working?" His chiseled jaw clenched, his bold eyes narrowed. "You off duty?" His leaned forward. His eyes darted around the taxi. "Where is your license?"

License? Damn. Derek was going to have to repaint the Old Girl to anything but yellow after I got squared away with the big guy and his wad of cashola tomorrow.

"What's with all the questions?" I turned back around and readjusted my clothes, and then ran my hands down my hair. I reached over and dug deep in my bag to get my lip gloss. Quickly I added a little shine to my pout.

"Well? License?" he asked again.

"Yes. I'm on duty." I might as well let him ride along since I was driving home and I could charge him anything I wanted. And he was easy to look at. "I just got the car back from the shop so my license hasn't been hung up yet."

The lies just kept coming. Piling up, like they had done when I was younger. My stomach started to hurt, my head ached. What was wrong with me? Why did trouble always seem to follow me wherever I went?

"Good. I need a lift to Walnut Grove." He settled back into the seat and propped his elbow up on the window frame.

I caught myself staring back at him a couple of times. There was no one—and I mean no one—that looked as good as him in Walnut Grove. Not even Johnny Delgato. Close, but not quite. I shook Johnny's good looks and bad boy image from my head. This was no time to think about him.

The guy's chest filled the navy button down, but not too much like the muscle guy before. His hair was black and silky straight with just the right amount of gel to give it a little spike in the front. He was well manicured and if I didn't know better, it looked like his eyebrows could've been professionally waxed. He looked to be in his late twenties or early thirties.

Sigh. A small amount of air rushed out of my lips. I pursed them shut and slid my eyes back to the road when I saw him looking back in the rearview at me.

"Do you live in Louisville?" His eyes danced in amusement. I bet he was used to women staring at him.

"No. I live in Walnut Grove." Okay, idle chit-chat was good. Maybe he was single.

"How long have you lived there?" He looked back out the window bringing his fingers to his chin and keeping his elbow in the window.

"All my life." Hearing those words escape my mouth left me sad. It was true. I'm not sure how I got to the orphanage but all of my memories were there, with Trixie.

I glanced down at my watch. It was lunch time and I was sure Trixie was home watching "Judge Judy". She loved trying to figure out what Judy was going to do before the gavel came down. The last thing I needed was for her to see me traipsing through town in a yellow car with a stranger—albeit hot stranger—in the back seat.

"I bet your parents are proud that you stayed around in a small town like Walnut Grove," he said.

His voice had a hint of a northern accent. Definitely not a twang like mine.

"Parents?" I bit my lip. "Um, yea, they are proud."

I tapped the wheel. I had had enough of his questions. I flipped on the old stereo and started to punch the little black buttons hoping the radio would magically work.

"Have you been a taxi driver for long?"

"Not really," I replied and reached over to turn up the volume a little more before I hit the dash. Loud static filled the car.

"Is this the most popular song around here?" he asked about the static and broke into a wide, open smile.

It was high time I turned the questioning on him. I flipped the radio off.

"We don't have great reception on these roads." I gestured to the curves ahead.

He arched his brows.

I took my hand and ran it over my brows. With the cash Tony gave me, I would be able to get them waxed. I made a mental note to stop by Shear Illusions to make an appointment with Kim Banta.

"So, why are you in town Mr…."

"Jackson. Jax Jackson." His eyes narrowed and the right corner of his lip slightly turned up.

Jax Jackson. Man, did that sound like a movie star's name. Definitely older than late twenties. There were smile lines on the outside of his eyes that formed as his smile deepened.

"Are you here to look into Walnut Grove hosting the Underworld Music Festival?" I glanced back.

He cleared his throat. "Umm, that."

"You are!" I nearly ran the car off the road before I cut to the left bringing us back on the pavement. "I knew you had an accent. Are you from New York City?"

My heart pounded a mile a minute. This was my big break. This was how I could redeem myself and save my job with Morty.

"Are you here to see Porty Morty?" I asked.

"Porty who?" He unzipped his duffle bag and took out a small spiral notepad.

"Oh, Morty Shelton. We all call him Porty Morty because of the you know." I waved one hand in the air.

"No I don't know." He continued to write something in that little pad of his.

"Porty Morty Port-A-Lets. His business." I shrugged.

"You said Shelton?" He glanced up, a serious look on his face.

"Yes. Morty Shelton," I repeated myself. "He is who I worked for before I got fired and I was the one who went to New York and left you the note. Only I didn't know you, Jax Jackson, was who I needed to see. The contest didn't give a name." I smiled, feeling all warm and fuzzy. I was so excited that I couldn't shut my own mouth up. "I'm just glad you got the note. Sorry about the bubble gum wrapper. It was all I could find."

"What note was that again?" he asked.

I looked back at him as he scribbled away. He sure did ask a lot of questions.

"I had found the contact information of the Underworld Music Festival on your contest ad in the Vogue magazine I had gotten down at the Food Town Grocery Store on Oak Street. I can't afford the magazine on my low budget, but I knew once you heard of our town that you'd come here to check it out. So I splurged and bought it. Granted, I had to put back the milk for Henrietta, but she likes water." I reached over and grabbed my bag. I dug my hand deep down in the big hobo and pulled out the wrinkled contest ad I had kept in there and handed it to him over my shoulder. "Anyway, I worked at Porty Morty's and my job was to go around to different events like family reunions, bass fishing tournaments, revivals, hog killings…"

"Hog killings?" he asked. He put the ad on his thigh and used his hands to unwrinkle it.

"Yeah, we have a lot of those around here. You know," I kept my hands on ten and two and carefully took the last set of curves going into Walnut Grove, "the men kill the hog while the women get a big pot of boiling water ready to cook him. They got to have some place to pee. I mean go to the bathroom. Anyway, I knew if I could get the festival to come to Walnut Grove then we could turn a big profit at Porty Morty's and I wouldn't have to work so hard for a pay check."

I pinched my lips together. It was true. I was so tired of going to every single family in Walnut Grove and asking if they had any family functions coming up so we could rent to them a port-a-let. It wasn't great money but it was money. The way I saw it, I would make a big commission on a festival. They would need hundreds of shitters.

"Think about it," I was going to sell Jax Jackson right here in this car. "Walnut Grove is a perfect place for your festival. It's close to the airport and a big city. Well, big for

Kentucky. And it's near the river which makes a great backdrop for any band. Perfect if you ask me."

"Yeah, perfect for all sorts of things," he added in a lower, huskier tone.

"So are you going to hire us?"

"Us? I thought you said Porty Morty fired you."

"Yes, but if you sign on the dotted line, maybe I can get my job back. Maybe you can give Morty a good report about me." My heart flipped. It seemed things were turning around.

"We'll see. I need to go to…," he hesitated and flipped through his little notebook, "The Windmill Hotel."

I looked back down at my watch and noticed the time was now twenty minutes after twelve. "Nope. Can't do that."

"Can't or won't?"

"Can't. Louie isn't up yet." I turned off Route 25 and down Grove Street. The row of small dotted houses lined the right side. They were beat up and broken down. They were still occupied but shouldn't be.

I watched Jax's expression when we passed. His mouth was gaped open. I bet he had never seen such a thing, especially since he had come clear from New York City.

Washing machines on the front porches, old couches with springs sticking out of them like Jack-in-the-box, and tires lying all about.

Making a quick right onto Oak Street and a fast left on Main Street brought us to the heart of Walnut Grove.

"Who's Louie?" he asked. His face set in perplexities.

"Louie Pelfrey. He's the owner of the Windmill." I guess I wasn't good at driving a taxi or meeting strangers. I talked to Jax like he was from around here and knew everyone. Little did I realize I was going to have to explain the goings on around Walnut Grove. "You will know Louie when you see him. He is as big around as he is tall. Nice guy. He is the Krispy Kreme delivery guy. It's speculated whether people get all of the Krispy Kremes they ordered when Louie delivers."

"Why wouldn't he be at the hotel?" Jax tugged on the sleeve of his button down and caused it to expose a big black industrial looking watch. The Iron Man kind. "It's after noon."

"He has to get up awfully early to make his deliveries so he likes to go back to bed until at least one thirty," I said and pulled up in front of The Cracked Egg Café.

Gia pressed her face up against the large bay window and looked out at the street directly at me and Jax.

"We can grab a coffee at The Cracked Egg while you wait. You hungry?" I asked and stuck my hand out, "Oh, and you owe me one hundred dollars for the ride."

"One hundred dollars? Now I can't afford to eat." Jax let out a heavy sigh. He didn't try to hide the fact he was a little unhappy with the taxi fare and the sudden change in his plans.

"You needed to get here and I was your only way. Plus, if you made a reservation with Louie, he should've told you." I turned the car off and felt around for my phone. "Bastard," I whispered under my breath when I remembered my last passenger had thrown my phone out of the window.

"Excuse me?" Jax leaned forward, tossing a Ben Franklin my way. "Did you call me a bastard?"

"Not you." I shook my head trying to erase what I had said.

"Louie?" There he went with the questions again.

"Um." I had to think about that one because I probably would've called Louie a bastard. Not today. "The guy I just dropped off before you got in."

"Friend of yours?" He lingered with his hand on the door handle.

"Far from it," I quipped, grabbed my big hobo bag and jumped out of the car. "Come on, Gia is dying in there." I stuck the one hundred dollars in my bag.

The Cracked Egg did a hell of a business because the town square was the heart of Walnut Grove with the courthouse and Friendship Baptist Church in the center.

Two things Southerners loved: small town politics and their church.

The Cracked Egg was always busy at lunch. There were café tables dotted in the middle of the diner and booths that outlined the perimeter. The diner was a million years old, well, not a million but old. The booths still had the old time music players on the tables that didn't work. Gia's dad claimed it added to the authenticity of the diner.

"Just pick a seat and sit," I told him and pointed to the counter. "I'm going to grab a seat up there. Let me know when you are ready."

Every since Gia and I met in Kindergarten, I had been coming to the diner and sitting in the exact same spot. The stools were so much fun. Gia and I would twirl for hours.

Mr. Chiconi, Gia's dad, stopped yelling at us to stop after we continually didn't listen.

"Who's the hottie?" Gia chomped on her gum and slightly tilted her head toward Jax who was in ear shot.

"Jax Jackson." He put his hand out over my shoulder for Gia to shake. "I'm here on business and I have to say you have a very nice taxi service here in Walnut Grove. Much better than New York City."

"Taxi?" Gia snorted and pulled the pen out of her up-do. She hated how her dad made her put her hair up on top of her head. She had so much curly black hair that she had to use two ponytail holders and several bobby pins just to keep it in place. She always claimed she had to get up an hour early just to fix her hair. She looked at me. "We got a taxi in town?"

Me, I mouthed and with the slip of my finger, I pointed to myself. Only I wasn't sly enough. Jax saw me.

"You aren't a taxi?" Jax's mouth dropped wide open. "I want my money back."

"Hey," I put my hands in the air. "I never said, nor did my car say I was a taxi. You are the one who jumped in."

"What about the guy you dropped off before me?" he asked.

"What about him?" I asked. "What it is to you? He's a client."

"What client? I thought you got fired?" Gia put her two cents in.

"I'll take a coffee with two creamers and three sugars," I told Gia. "The free coffee," I reminded her of her offer from this morning.

"You gonna give me part of that hundred?" she asked with a shit-eating grin on her face. She flipped the white coffee cup over and placed it back in the matching saucer before she reached behind her and got the freshly brewed pot of coffee. She poured. "You can buy us a round of drinks tonight."

"Tonight!" I gasped. I hit the palm of my hand on my head. "I forgot all about tonight."

"Don't you dare." Gia shook her head. "It took a lot for Carmine to get Antonio to come down here from Cincinnati to go on a date with you."

"It's bowling. Not a date." I reminded her that it was her idea, not mine. "You said that we needed to add a bowler to the team. But I'll be there."

“So Jax Jackson, you in town for business?” Gia didn’t care about personal space. She was always up in everyone’s craw.

“What makes you think it’s business?” Jax was good at dodging questions by asking his own in his answers. “Maybe I’m just passing through.”

“First off,” Gia chomped, “passing through is generally at night and here for supper. Secondly, you hopped into Laurel’s fake taxi to get a ride here.”

“And you are staying at the Windmill.” I added my two cents before I lifted the lid off of the pie dish and helped myself to a piece of the best apple pie this side of the Mississippi.

“So tell me Jax Jackson, why are you in Walnut Grove?” There was a deep-set suspicion in her eyes.

“He’s with the Underworld Music Festival,” I blurted out before I stuck a fork full of pie in my mouth.

“You are?” Gia pulled back. Her eyes narrowed. “I told you Carmine said they’d have it all worked out in three weeks. But Carmine didn’t say anything about someone coming today.”

“And Carmine tells you everything.” There was something that wasn’t adding up here. It was true. Carmine never kept anything from Gia. "He didn't tell you about Morty firing me either," I reminded her.

"Something's fishy." Gia smacked her hand on the counter and rushed over to where the cash register sat. She grabbed the phone off the wall and pulled the phone cord up over her head so the server could go under it. "Carmine!" I heard Gia scream into the phone.

"Oh no. Someone is getting into trouble." Jax laughed. "Who's Carmine and what did she mean by three weeks?"

"Mind your own business," Gia yelled over her shoulder at Jax.

"So what's good here?" Jax picked up the laminated menu and gave it the once over.

"Everything," I said and picked up my cup of coffee. Out of my peripheral vision I could see Jax Jackson was staring at me.

## Chapter Seven

“Don’t forget about your date!” Gia yelled over the lunch crowd as she hustled her butt to get people their lunches.

After she gave Carmine the business, she didn’t have time to chit-chat with Jax and me. He ordered the bacon, lettuce and tomato double decker and so did I. Oh, and extra fries.

“That was good.” Jax patted his belly. He checked his watch as we stepped outside. “Do you think Louie is up yet?”

“He should be.” Walking to the car, I retrieved the Benjamin from the bottom of my hobo and handed it to him. “I can’t take your money. I’ll take you to the Windmill.”

I held on to the corner of the bill while he tugged on the other end.

“Are you going to let go?” He jerked a little harder. “I guess I owe you something for bringing me here. What did the other guy give you?”

"Why are you so curious about the other guy in my taxi?" I would understand if Derek or Gia asked me these questions but not this guy. This stranger.

"Taxi? Aren't you using the term loosely?" His smart ass comment made me laugh.

"Get in." I opened the door and plopped down. "Louie should be there by now."

Jax and I didn't say another word until we got to the Windmill, which was only less than a half mile down Main Street.

"This is it?" Jax looked frightened.

There was a broken down windmill in front of the hotel with a half lit sign attached to it. A couple of the blades were missing, a few were dangling. The slightest bit of wind made the old thing creak and groan. It was a perfect site for one of those creepy thriller movies.

"The one and only." I pulled the old Belvedere into the lot and stopped right in front of the glass window where big Louie was happily sitting.

"I see what you mean by big Louie." Jax moved his head back and forth as though he was surveying the place.

"It might not look like much from the outside, but it's super clean on the inside. Sally Bent cleans all the rooms.

She's a freak." I took a deep breath and corrected what I had said about Sally. "Neat freak."

Sally Bent was another girl in the orphanage. Louie's parents wanted a girl so they came and adopted Sally. It was a real shame. Not to her, but to me. Sally Bent cleaned a toilet better than anyone I had ever seen. She loved doing all the chores, but when she left, Trixie said I had to do it. You need to learn how to cook and clean so you can get married one day. Little did we realize no one wanted to date me, let alone marry me.

No one in Walnut Grove. Given my background, I could hardly blame them. But I was on the upswing. I could feel it. Plus I had been on my best behavior over the last five or so years.

Damn. Wasn't that long enough to prove I was good?

"Sally Bent, huh?" Jax hesitated before he opened the door. "Well, Laurel, it was a pleasure."

"All mine." I smiled and watched him walk up to the window. His backside was just as nice as the front. "Yep, pleasure is all mine," I said under my breath before I took off toward Cow's Lick Creamery.

I was in the mood for some of their homemade raspberry chocolate chunk ice cream. I still had a few hours to kill before I could officially go back home. Even though I lived alone, Trixie somehow knew if I was home early or late.

"Dang." I hit the wheel when the only light in town turned red.

The door opened and someone jumped in.

"I need to go to Porty Morty's." The woman slammed the door and adjusted her cutoff jeans before she tried to pull down the cowl neck crop top that was so popular in the 90's. Her long grey hair was covered in a tin foil hat. "Laurel London?"

"Trixie!" I was just as shocked to see her as she was to see me. "What in the hell is on your head?"

I wasn't about to ask about the clothes. I already knew where those had come from…the orphanage. It wasn't a big secret and everyone around town knew Trixie didn't buy her own clothes. She just wore all the orphans' hand-me-downs.

To this day she still refused to buy clothes that were not only in the current trend, but that were to fit her age of seventy years old.

"Watch your language! Who the hell's car is this? Gee Laurel, please don't tell me you stole it." She jumped out of the back of the car, ran around it, and then hopped in the front seat with me. It was sort of like playing the Chinese fire drill game but with a slightly crazy old lady. "I got a phone call from Mr. Chiconi." She did the sign of the cross.

"Why do you do that? He's not dead and we aren't Catholic." I rolled my eyes.

"His father is dead. Bless his soul. He was a good man." She tsked. "By the looks of things, he's right and I wasn't so sure about Sally Bent's claim of you being a woman of the night, but now I'm starting to believe her too. It's those aliens, I'm telling you."

Trixie dipped her head, shot her eyes to the sky and looked out of the front windshield.

"Lady of the night? As in prostitute? Aliens?" I questioned. Who was she calling lady of the night? She was the one in the skimpy outfit. "Are you drinking in the middle of the day?" I asked.

I'm going to get that Sally Bent for good this time. I made a mental note.

"Mr. Chiconi said you were driving some big yellow car and a man was in the car. A stranger." Her eyes were big and blue. Her skin was fair and with very few wrinkles. I was sure it was from all the sunscreen she used and doused the orphans with. When they came up with the slogan, big things come in small packages, I believe they had Trixie in mind. She was a spitfire. "Where is he?" She pulled a knife out of her hot pink handbag—that I was positive came from the Salvation Army drop box—and slashed it through the air.

There were many times we'd stake out the drop-off site of the Salvation Army donation dumpster. Not only was Sally Bent a good bathroom cleaner, she was tiny and would fit right in the dumpster. Trixie would send Sally sailing over the top and into the pile of donated stuff.

Sally always came out with all sorts of great items that we'd take back to the orphanage and wear.

"Whoa. Where's who?" I continued past the creamery. My sudden appetite for the raspberry chocolate chunk went south. I had to tell Trixie about my bad fortune of being fired.

"The stranger." Trixie jabbed her pointy finger on my shoulder. I grimaced in pain. "I'll chop off his penis!"

"Listen, I'm not doing anything illegal." It was time to come clean. I didn't want anyone's body parts being chopped off. "Shouldn't you be home watching 'Judge Judy'?" I asked buying time.

I pulled over into the Dollar Store parking lot. I knew when I told her about me losing my job, she was not going to be happy.

"Don't change the subject." She looked out the window, craning her neck to see where we were. "I don't need laundry powder. Why are we at the Dollar Store?"

Growing up with Trixie and in the orphanage, you quickly learned how to get the best deals and how to stretch your dollar. The Dollar Store on Fifth Street had the best prices on laundry powder. Fiddle and Sons Meats had the best meat and potato salad. Dealing with them was an adventure I could do without.

Fiddle and Sons was next to Porty Morty's. They served lunch and it was convenient when I was at work. On most days, Morty would send me over to get him a hot ham and cheese for lunch. The sons of Fiddle and Sons were twins, Adam and Alex, and they are my age. Gia and I aptly named them Fiddle Dee and Fiddle Dum. They were on my bowling team so I had the pleasure of seeing them on a weekly basis.

"I have to tell you something and I don't want to be driving when I tell you." I put the car in park and turned slightly toward her in my seat.

"Oh no. I've got a chill just waiting for you to tell me you've been renting a room over at the Windmill for the nasty men to visit. Wait until I get my hands on Louie Pelfrey for giving you a room!" She balled her fists up.

"Oh my God!" My frustration level was peeking. "I'm not a prostitute and I'm not driving around strange men."

"Morty is going to have to give your other car back or else," Trixie warned.

"That's what I have to tell you." I reached over and grabbed her hand. "Morty fired me a few days ago and I'm currently working on getting the job back."

"What?" Trixie mouth flew open.

"He said something about downsizing. But Carmine didn't know anything about it." I spewed like a volcano. "I didn't do anything to get fired. Scout's honor." I put my hand in the air after I used my finger to cross my heart. "In fact the stranger Mr. Chiconi saw with me is in town for the big event I had been working on for over a year. He needed a ride from the Airport Hotel because he got in late and spent the night there. He is going to spend the rest of his trip in town so staying at the Windmill made much more sense for him."

Trixie put her knife in the glove box, slammed it closed, and then crossed her arms. I could see a twinge of disappointment on her face. She adjusted her tin foil hat.

"I bet they are coming." She tapped the homemade hat. "Strange things are happening and I have to take care of you."

"You take great care of me." I reached over and squeezed her hand.

"Who is coming?" I asked, questioning the deer-in-the-headlights look in her eyes.

"I saw it on the SyFy channel." She nodded, as sure as shit she was right. "The aliens are coming because everyone is going crazy around this town."

"Aliens?" My eyes narrowed.

"Yes. That documentary said that if you put tin foil on your head, they can't zap into your brain." Crinkle, crinkle. The hat made sounds as she smoothed her hand over it to mold better to her head. "I bet they got to Morty. Thank God I made you one before I left home because I knew if you were prostituting, they had gotten you too." She dug deep in her pink bag and pulled out another tin foil hat and slapped it on my head.

"I don't think so." I reached up to take it off and she slapped my hand away.

"Don't you dare take that off," she warned me.

"Just listen," I begged her. "You know when I went to New York to meet the publicity people." I didn't mention the fact she's been mad as hell that I did. "Well, they are here to look at Walnut Grove for that big music festival. It would bring so much income to the town, not to mention that I brought them here."

I took the tin foil off my head.

"No aliens are coming here." I smiled to try to ease her mind even though my mind was a jumbled mess. "Don't watch the SyFy channel anymore," I ordered her.

"You think Morty will give you your job back?" Trixie asked. "He is the only one in this town I could get to give you a job. A real job, Laurel."

"I know." I felt ice spreading through my stomach. The last thing I ever wanted to do was disappoint Trixie. After all she had done for me. "But this car is all mine."

"It's nothing to brag about," Trixie snarled.

"No, but it's mine and Morty gave me fifteen hundred dollars which I plan to give to Pastor Wilson to pay for the next three months." That was a lie. But it wasn't a bad idea.

"I'm glad to see you are thinking into the future." Trixie wrung her hands. "I'm going to go see Morty and knock some sense into him."

"No. Let me handle things. I'm a grown woman," I reminded her, even though some would argue I still had a lot of growing up to do.

"And that is supposed to make me feel better?" Trixie was good at making smart remarks, one thing I loved about her.

"No, but let me handle it. If I don't get my job back with the Underworld Music Festival people in town, then you can give him a piece of your mind." I smiled. She smiled back. I reached over and patted her hand. "I don't need the knife."

"Oh yes you do." She rubbed the dash like it was going to give good juju to the sharp metal blade and keep it safe. "Especially if you are driving around some man that we do not know." She jabbed her finger in her chest. "I do not know. Put that hat on."

There was no sense in arguing with her. When she had her mind set, it was set.

"Let's get you home," I suggested and stuck the tin foil hat on my head to make her happy.

"I do need to catch up on my soap operas." She straightened her shoulders and put her hands in her lap. She seemed a little more satisfied.

## Chapter Eight

After I dropped Trixie off, I decided to go home and check on Henrietta.  What else did I have to do?

The quickest way to get home from Trixie's house was to take River Road and cut down Third Street to turn right on Main Street just in case the raspberry chocolate chunk ice cream craving hit. The only thing that hit me was a death stare from Pastor Wilson who was standing on the corner of Third and Main talking to a few locals.

"Damn," I grunted.

I had told Trixie I was going to give that money to Pastor Wilson and I knew she would check on me. It was in my best interest to keep my word and now was the time. Otherwise I might forget the urgency and spend it on foolish things…like ice cream.

I pulled off the side of the road and into a parking spot across the street from Cow's Lick and next to Friendship Baptist Church.

Out of the rearview mirror, I saw that Pastor did a double-take my way. Gracefully, he put his hands on the smalls of the locals' backs and guided them away from me.

I grabbed my hobo and jumped out of the Old Girl.

"Pastor! Pastor!" I screamed and jogged toward him. The louder I yelled the faster his legs moved.

The two locals turned around but he didn't.

When Pastor Wilson did turn around, all I could see was the same anger I had seen when I was fifteen years old when he called me a little blackmailer.

Every Christmas they would open their home to one lucky orphan from the orphanage and spoiled them with lavish gifts.

That one particular Christmas I was on my best behavior and I did want them to pick me, which they did. Once they got me home and sat me down, only then did I realize the rules they expected me to play by.

You will do a testimony in front of the church congregation at Christmas Eve service. You will tell them how great it is in our home and how thankful you are for us picking you. Plus you will ask to be baptized. You will write an article to the Walnut Grove paper saying how great the Wilsons are and the church made you feel so welcome. And you will smile the entire time doing it or we will take you right back to the orphanage where you can eat slop instead of a fine turkey meal on Christmas Day.

Instead of playing by their rules, I played by my own. Little did the Wilsons know that I had a natural knack for hacking, namely bank accounts. So after our "little chat," I happily agreed to be all grateful for the charity, but Laurel London didn't take no one's charity, not even a Baptist preacher. Their computer was right there in the guest bedroom. Prime picking for a con like me.

I did my magic. The next thing I knew, I was down at the local Wal-Mart picking up my online order with Derek…right there to give mc a hand.

So when I needed a place to live and he owned it, I reminded him of our little agreement that I wouldn't tell the world that he really didn't buy those gifts for the orphanage that particular Christmas and his good religious image would be shattered. Now I was happy to say I was the Pastor and Rita's newest renter.

Granted. He called me a blackmailer. I said it was just God's way of helping me get my own place.

"Pastor, if I didn't think you were a good Christian man, I'd think you were ignoring me." I always knew how to give a good dig to someone in his position.

"Yes Laurel, what can I help you with?" Ahem, he cleared his throat and clasped his hands in front of him and rocked back on his heels.

I looked up. The sun covered his face. He was a slender man. Always wore a suit that was either grey or black. And he stood six foot three. I came to his shoulders. He had thinning hair and a pointy nose.

I took the money Morty had given me out of my hobo and handed it over to Pastor Wilson.

"What's this?" He looked perplexed.

"I wanted to pay three months rent up front." I smiled and turned around knowing he was shitting his pants. I walked back to the car.

Every month I was a tad bit late on my rent and every month he would send Rita to collect from me. He was too chicken shit to face me. I guess I just haven't gotten over the fact that he used orphans to create his own good guy image. What man of God did that?

"Thank you, Laurel." Pastor's voice was unsure at first but escalated. "You sure are a good tenant."

I smiled, even though he couldn't see it with my back turned. I had gotten his goat and he knew it just as much as

I did. I put my hand in the air and waved over my shoulder. At least I wouldn't be seeing him for three more months.

I jumped back in the car and headed north on Main and turned on Second Street. Friendship Baptist's parking lot was on the corner and next to that was the Walnut Grove Courthouse and next to that was the Walnut Grove Savings. Yes. The same bank I had gotten the money to pay for the pizza.

Funny how Pastor Wilson owned the building and the apartment on top.

"Home sweet home." I pulled into the furthest spot in the bank parking lot—where I was told I could park. The rest were for the bank customers.

I could hear Henrietta scratching at the door as I climbed the steel steps up to the efficiency.

I unlocked the door and pushed my way in.

"Hey girl."

Henrietta took off under the couch where I plopped down. "Momma has a new gig which means you won't go hungry."

When I lost my job at Porty Morty's, Henrietta and Trixie were the first two people I thought of. So Henrietta wasn't a real person, but she was all I had.

I pulled my hobo closer to me and looked inside for the cash from the muscled client from this morning.

Carefully I counted each hundred like it was a piece of fine China. The cash Morty gave me was a three week paycheck.

"One, two, three, four, five." My eyes got bigger as the number went up. "Twelve, thirteen, fourteen," my voice escalated, "two thousand dollars!"

I jumped up off the couch, waving the money in the air.

"Whoop whoop! How you doin'?" I asked the cash like it was going to answer. I started kissing the bills. "All for a little ride to and fro."

I reached for my bag to grab my phone to set the alarm for tomorrow morning to make sure I had plenty of time to pick up muscle man…money man when he told me to.

"Damn." I threw the purse back on the couch when I remembered my phone was gone. It looked like a little bit of this money was going to have to go toward a new phone. Oh well, hopefully he really would give me a little more cash when I picked him up in the morning.

After counting the money one more time, Henrietta and I decided to watch a little TV before I had to get ready for bowling night.

Gia, Carmine, Derek, the Fiddle twins and I were on a bowling team, Here For The Beer, at Lucky Strikes Lanes on the corner of Grove and Oak Streets. Gia claimed we needed another player since all the other teams had a round number of eight and asked Carmine's best friend from Louisville, Antonio, to come down and play as a sit in.

That's what she told him.

She told me that I was going to be set up on a date with him. If he was anything like Carmine, she could forget it.

I opted to wear my skinny jeans with my white tee-shirt and sneakers. The bowling shoes were ancient ones and nothing I could wear would look good with them. To dress up the tee, I put on a big silver beaded necklace and matching bracelet along with my watch. I ran a brush through my hair and a couple of swipes of mascara to show off my grayish blue eyes. Sometimes when I look in the mirror, I feel like I can see right through them because they look transparent when I wear mascara.

Everyone always complimented me on my eyes, always asking which side of the family I got them from.

Unfortunately I was never able to answer that question. I would smile and say thank you.

Trixie always told me that I was beautiful but my actions made me ugly.

It was a nice night. I gave Henrietta a can of food and grabbed my bag. I decided to walk the block over to Lucky Strikes. No sense in using up my gas. I tried to stay away from the Gas-N-Go as much as I could.

Lucky Strikes' large bowling pin sign flickered on and off with a buzzing sound. No matter where you were on Main Street, you could see the pin. Owners Bud and Sheila McKay said it was too expensive to fix all the neon lights. Everyone knew that Monday night was bowling night. Most of Walnut Grove was there.

"Evening." I smiled and pushed my way through the crowd to lane three.

Normally I would grab a beer on my way over, but if I batted my eyes at Antonio maybe I'd get a free beer.

The gang was all there plus two extras. One could only be Antonio because the other was Jax Jackson.

"What are you doing here?" I tried to breathe normally as my heart sped up. Just looking at him made my heart race, something that had never happened to me before. Antonio sure wasn't doing it for me.

Antonio looked like he had eaten a little too much pasta and forgot to exercise after. Not that dating a heavier guy was beneath me or anything, but he had to be able to go the distance in bed. Antonio didn't look like he could go from here to the bar without breaking a sweat. There goes the free beer.

"Beer?" Jax smiled while shoving a beer bottle in my face.

"Be nice Laurel. He was sitting at the bar all by himself so I asked him to join us." Gia was sitting on the orange plastic bench, bent over lacing up the generic bowling shoes.

Something in my con artist gut told me something was fishy.

I leaned over just enough to take the beer and just enough for Jax to hear me whisper, "It takes a con to know a con and you aren't fooling me, Jax Jackson." My heart was being fooled by him. Definitely being fooled. But my head wasn't. I did the "I got my eyes on your gesture" with my fingers.

The arrogant devil shot me a smile and winked. Immediately I went over to the ball rack where Gia was testing out every single bowling ball. It was the same crap every week. First she'd pick up a ball, put her fingers in it, hold it up to eye level and give it a good once over before she pretended to bowl with it. She did this to every single ball in the rack. And every single time she picked the purple one, size ten.

"There is something going on with him," I whispered in her ear as she was eyeing the blue ball with gold flecks all over it.

"Who cares?" She did her pretend roll.

"One of these days you are going to let go of that thing and it'll go right through the display case." I pointed to the glass case where there were shoes, gloves, balls, and Lucky Strike paraphernalia on sale. Bud was hunched over leaning on his elbows on the counter. He had a piece of straw sticking out of his bearded mouth. He looked so grizzly, you couldn't see his lips. "Bud and Sheila will not like that."

"Why don't you leave Jax Jackson well enough alone and go hang out with Antonio?" Gia got all sassy by snapping her finger in the air and rotating her neck like she had a crook in it.

"Have you seen Antonio?" I asked.

"So he's gained a few." Gia chomped her gum and looked over at Antonio. "Okay, a lot. He's a nice guy."

"Fine." I shrugged and headed over to the shoe counter where Shelia was passing out the lovely accessory.

"Good evening, Laurel. How have you been?" Sheila had on her skintight v-neck shirt with the bowling balls on it and her black leggings.

"Good. I need a size eight please." I smiled. "Your hair looks nice."

"Oh that." She grinned and pushed her fingertips in the sides of her flaming red hair. "Yea, Bud doesn't like it too good, but I do. Makes me a little frisky if you know what I mean." She winked before she went to retrieve my size eights.

What was it with the winking around here?

"Unfortunately, I don't know what you mean." I gulped before I took the shoes. The idea of my feet going into something where thousands of feet have gone, kind of gave me the creeps every single time. I have to physically make my mind not think about it on bowling night. Sheila claims she cleans them real good. I've seen what she means by real good and it came in an aerosol can. Still not good enough for me. I carried a can of Lysol in my hobo just for instances like bowling night.

"You mean that hot guy with the accent isn't with you?" Sheila pointed her long lean finger with the red hot painted fake fingernail toward my group. "I heard you've been carting him around in a fancy new car before stopping at the Windmill to do God knows what."

"Oh my God!" I grabbed the ugly shoes out of Sheila's other hand and marched back to the group, anger boiled my blood seeing Jax Jackson in one of our Here For The Beer tie-dyed shirts. It was all I needed to put me over the edge. "What is he doing in our shirt?"

Steam rolled out of my ears.

"Antonio, this is Laurel." Gia ignored my question by smiling and turning toward Antonio.

"Is this the babe that's gonna sleep with me?" A snarky grin tipped his lips making my stomach curl. "I thought you said she was hot?" He turned to Carmine who shrugged.

"Trust me," I put very little distance between my nose and his, "I don't need help finding a date and he sure wouldn't smell like bologna like you do."

Alex Fiddle pushed his glasses back up on the bridge of his nose. He swallowed hard. "Man, why did you have to go and piss her off?"

"Yea, don't you know her history?" Adam Fiddle ran his hands through his short black hair. These days the twins were wearing their hair shorter on the sides and a little longer on the top with a side part. I had to say that it was working for them. The older they got, the cuter they got.

The Fiddles were always a set of scrawny little guys. We, the orphan kids, always told them to steal some of their dad's meat and eat.

"Do you think I'd waste my time driving down here on that?" Antonio's nose curled as he looked my body up and down. "I like a little more meat on my girl's bones. You know?" He did a little air grinding, making my stomach curl at the thought. "Something to hold on to."

The guys chuckled.

I inhaled deeply and stood up straight, shook my hair behind my head with my chin up in the air and grabbed the bottle of beer out of Jax's hands, chugging down what he had left in it. Normally I wouldn't have anything to do with back wash and drinking after strangers, but there wasn't anything normal about this situation.

"Let's get this game going." I tossed the bottle in the trash. I pointed directly at Jax. "Get me another one."

The group dropped to silent, barely breathing. I grabbed the Lysol can out of my bag and sprayed the insides of the shoes. I threw the can to Gia before I gripped my bowling ball. I took a couple of steps forward toward the lane. I cupped my wrist and quickly opened it at the top of my swing. I used the old plant and pull method for more leverage on the ball because the speed and power helped me get out my frustration.

Slowly I turned around and walked back toward the team with my ears on full alert. I knew it was a great bowl and a strike was in my foreseeable future. The whiz of the ball struck the pins, knocking all of them down.

"Damn." Jax leaned to the right to look over my shoulder at the strike. He leaned back staring at me—his mouth open.

I walked right past him and grabbed the beer he had gotten me.

“Close your mouth.” I heard Gia say to him. “She’s a cranker.” Gia referred to the delivery style I had chosen to do.

“She’s something,” Jax said in a little sarcastic tone. “I never bowl. I’m terrible.”

Derek walked up. He surveyed the group and did a head nod Carmine’s way who head nodded back. Some sort of guy talk was going on because the two of them shrugged.

Derek was always late on Monday night because after lunch he had to drive to class and would make it just in time for him to be the last bowler on the team, in the first round.

It was apparent he felt the same way I did about Jax. Derek plopped down in the plastic seat next to me and dropped his shoes making us all look after they smacked down on the old tile floor.

“What’s he doing here?” Derek asked in a hushed whisper. He didn’t look at me. He took off his shoes and slipped the bowling shoes on.

“How do you know him?” I asked back when Jax was out of earshot. He was next to bowl.

I couldn't help but smile when he crossed the foul line and the alarm sounded throughout Lucky Strikes. All the other teams looked and started to jab each other in pleasure. Everyone wanted to beat Here For The Beer, especially since all the other teams were members of the local AARP.

"Trixie called and told me you were prostituting. Then she called back because she said you weren't prostituting. Then I grabbed a BLT to go from The Cracked Egg on my way to class and Gia happened to mention you were in there with some stranger that you conned into thinking your car was a taxi." He clenched his jaws. There was no forgiveness in his eyes. "What happened to Quick Copy? I thought you were trying to be on the level when I gave you that car."

"I am." Damn, Gia. Her loose lip always got me in trouble.

I snuck a peek over at her. Her face was flush. It was apparent she knew he was reading me my Miranda Rights about my apparent bad decision of picking up a stranger and how I could have been killed, left for dead, and not found in years.

In the background, I took pleasure when I saw Jax had a split in order to get a spare. Newbie.

"He is the one who needed a ride and I wasn't going to do it for free since I have no job. Gas is expensive and I swear that Baxter Thacker is charging me more than other customers." I jabbed his bicep. "That is who you need to investigate first when you get your badge, or whatever it is that you get. Highway robbery I tell you!"

I had to get the heat off me.

Ugh. I inwardly groaned when I saw Jax's ball spin and whirl, hitting the ten pin and whipping it to the other side, knocking down the seven pin.

"Oh! I'm next." I shrugged and jumped up avoiding any more scolding from Derek.

Along the way I passed Jax who was strutting back to the group because of his little fake "I'm not a good bowler" act.

"Lucky bowl I guess." He shrugged. He smiled when I glared at him. The power of his gaze sent my heart into a twirly whirl—like those little helicopters that fell from trees. I swallowed hard. "Get another strike," he said.

"She will." Derek stood up. His legs were planted in a cop stance. His arms crossed.

Jax stopped. I bit my lip and didn't look back at them. Derek was going to have my back no matter what. I bet he was using his cop instincts to detect Jax Jackson's shit, just like I had.

Yep…Derek and I were cut from the same cloth, which was going to make him a great cop.

As the evening progressed the night got a little better. Antonio left when he figured out I wasn't going to do him any favors. I told Carmine and Gia to butt out of my love life. Henrietta was all I needed.

"Who's the hottie mctotty?" Norma Allen, the cranker for the Holy Rollers, was eyeing Jax up and down.

"Just a fill in," I mumbled over the seats.

The Holy Rollers were the old blue-haired women who made up the bible group that met in the undercroft of the Friendship Baptist Church and the same women in charge of preparing all the food that was consumed after a funeral.

They were spry and good bowlers. They were first in the league while we were in second. In fact, they spent any and all of their free time at Lucky Strikes. They were the league champs two years in a row.

"It doesn't matter who you have because we are going for the three-peat." Sharon Fasa held up three fingers in the air.

All the Holy Rollers chanted three-peat right along with her.

"So how did your lunch date with the hippie go the other day?" Gia popped down next to me when the twins took their turn to bowl. "I totally forgot to ask."

"Just because he drove a VW didn't make him a hippie." I jerked back toward Gia.

"He's never going to be happy with anyone you date." Gia raised a brow and glanced over my shoulder at Derek.

She was right. Any time I suggested a possible boyfriend, Derek always had something negative to say.

"It didn't work out." I turned my lip up. "On an upswing, I do have a cocktail date with Bob sometime this week."

Jax came over and sat down next to us. I did my best to ignore him.

"What happened to lunch?" Gia never liked me using the dating sites either.

She said that you never could be too sure about people and she was afraid I was going to get what she called "Laurel-napped."

"We are meeting up at Benny's. I'm sure I'll be fine." I took a swig of my beer. I nudged her with my elbow. "You're up."

Perfect timing too. I didn't want to have to explain why I decided to do cocktails instead of lunch.

The night went along just fine. Derek sat on one side, Jax on the other and I bounced all over the place trying to keep the peace with everyone, even the Holy Rollers when things started to heat up after they won the game. . .again.

"See y'all next week," I said after putting my ball back in the ball rack.

"Better luck next time." Sharon Fasa winked before she blew on her knuckles and pretended to polish them off on her shoulder.

"Did you see Trixie Turner with that foil on her head?" One of the other blue-hairs shook her head. "Crazy."

"Ignore them." Gia rushed over and grabbed me before I could go all ape shit on them. "Old people think they can say whatever they want. They are the crazy ones."

"I want to beat them." My blood pressure rose as I tried to keep it together. "Do not ask anyone else to join our team. Got it?" I jerked away and headed toward Shelia to return my shoes.

"Yeah. Fine," Gia called after me.

I put my shoes on the counter for Sheila and tried to get the hell out of Lucky Strikes. I didn't want to be interrogated by Derek. I didn't want to fight with old women. And I certainly didn't want to talk to Jax Jackson.

Poor Derek had an off game. He had several gutters, which I hadn't seen him do since we used to sneak out of the orphanage and sneak into Lucky Strikes in the middle of the night and play a couple rounds.

Derek didn't seem to care because he looked pretty content watching Jax's every move. Alex and Adam were pretty good bowlers. Carmine and Gia not so much, but Gia was my best friend and Carmine was her appendage. Jax Jackson didn't do so bad either, every frame he either had a strike or a spare. Too bad he's only here for the details of the festival. I hated to admit that the team could use him. He could be the extra member.

"Come on." Derek tilted his head toward his truck. He fiddled with his keys. "I'll give you a lift."

"Nah. It's a beautiful night." I ran my hand down his arm. "Thanks but it'll be good to walk off some of the beer calories."

"Suit yourself." Derek glanced around. The door swung open and Jax walked out. "You sure?"

"Yeah." I found it cute in a big brother kind of way that he was looking out for me. I waved bye to him after he jumped into the truck and sped off.

The parking lot was thinning out. I walked faster. Not that I was scared, but I could feel the stare of Jax Jackson.

"Hold up!" Jax yelled.

I ignored him until he jogged up next to me.

"You can drive me back to the Windmill." Jax assumed I was his taxi service while in town.

"I don't think so." I flung my bag over my shoulder and continued to walk outside. "Besides I walked."

The stars dotted the night sky. The temperature was perfect for a nice walk. It made me happy that I had chosen to walk instead of drive.

Gia and Carmine beeped when they drove up with the top down in their red Jeep Wrangler. Gia was lucky. Her parents gave her whatever she wanted. The Jeep was a present when she and Carmine had gotten married along with a house.

"You want to grab a beer from Benny?" Gia asked me and Jax.

I could see excitement at the prospect of something going on between me and Jax.

"No thanks. I'm tired." I waved her off and didn't even wait for Jax to answer.

"Call you tomorrow!" Gia screamed out, grabbing the rollover bar when Carmine peeled out of the parking lot.

"Wow!" Jax gasped and stood right in the middle of the parking lot as cars tried to pass him.

"Get out of the way." I shook my head and continued to walk. "You're going to get killed."

"Look at that sky." He rushed up next to me.

The smell of his cologne circled my head making me dizzy. I bet it was some high-dollar fancy New York City department store cologne. Definitely nothing they sold in the locked counter behind the make-up department at K-Mart.

I took a few quick breaths to keep me grounded.

"What?" I looked up thinking the stars were falling or something.

"I have never seen stars like that," he said. "Beautiful," he whispered so low, I barely heard him.

The moonlight dripped down on Jax like the night was meant for him. In the light, his hazel eyes shone like bits of gleaming porcelain.

"I…I'm glad you came to join us tonight. Too bad you can't come next week." There was a tingling in the pit of my stomach. I picked up the speed. For some reason I had to get out of his presence. It was making me lose all sense of control.

"Who said I was leaving anytime soon?" He kept pace with me. "Where are you going so fast? Got another date with the likes of Antonio?" He chuckled.

Abruptly I stopped, way before he noticed, knocking him into me. It only made him laugh more.

"Listen, I don't know who you are. But I do know that you are somehow watching me. You have been nasty ever since I picked your sorry ass up. Without me, you would have had to try to figure out your own way to Walnut Grove. I don't work for Porty Morty anymore. You can deal with him about the Underworld Music Festival yourself. So stop following me everywhere I go!" I jabbed my finger into his rock hard chest, which didn't help my stomach any. My mind whirled with wild images of what was under there. "Are you really with the festival? You better come clean or I will ask Morty myself."

He stared at me like he was assessing the situation. I ran across the street and through a couple of yards to make it over to Second Street. He ran after me. Right in front of the bank, Jax grabbed my arm. He twisted me around. His gaze was as soft as a caress. I jerked away.

"Laurel, I know you are on the mob payroll." His jaw clenched. His eyes slightly narrowed.

"Mob?" I threw my head back and a roar of laughter came out. "The Mob of Walnut Grove. Ohhhh!" I waved my hands out in front of me. "Yep, we use Lucky Strikes to make our plans. That is why I went ballistic when I saw you there." My words dripped with mockery of his idiotic remark. "Here For The Beer is our undercover name."

"I'm not kidding Laurel. I saw Trigger Finger Tony get out of your car. Not to mention the cash he threw at you. No less to keep your mouth shut." Jax was not joking. His eyes were hooded like those of a hawk. "You might as well go on and tell me. It will be much better in the long run. I'm sure we can get you a plea deal."

"Plea deal?" I chuckled but stopped when the seriousness of his words stung me. "Mob? You're joking right? Tony is definitely not a mob guy."

He reached around to his back pocket and took out his wallet. In a flip of his wrist, the wallet flung open exposing a large shiny metal badge that clearly read FBI across the top.

"Have you ever heard the FBI ever to joke?" His words left his mouth but to me it was in slow motion.

"Shit! Does that mean I have to give back the money?" I stomped around in a circle, not a care in the world that I had been an accomplice in some sort of mob interaction.

"You are admitting to it?" Jax Jackson threw questions at me left and right. "How do you know Trigger Finger Tony? When did he first contact you? Is there somewhere we can go because you are probably being watched." Jax looked around as if he was expecting someone to pop out with loaded guns.

"Whoa!" I put my hands out in front of me. "I don't know that guy. He was like you. He thought I was a taxi and paid me to take him to the Airport Hotel. That's it." I gripped the handle of my hobo bag and turned toward the bank. "Why is he called Trigger Finger Tony?"

The thought of his name struck a sudden fear in me. My mind twirled with all the images of famous mob families and their minions that offed people. Was Trigger Finger Tony in Walnut Grove to off someone?

"He is the head of the Cardozza family. That is why I know something big is going to go down." He waited to see my reaction.

My mind might have been going a million miles a minute, but my game face was on. Jax Jackson didn't realize he was standing right in front of the biggest con in Walnut Grove.

"How did he get the name?" I wasn't stupid.

Everyone and their brother had heard of the different mob names, most outrageous, and there were always reasons behind the name. Having the name Trigger Finger didn't sound so good to me and truly made one thing come to my mind…a gun.

"Let's say he loves piranhas. We, the FBI, always know when he's made a hit because his victims usually loose a finger or four to his family pets."

"Family pets?" I gulped, afraid to hear the answer.

"A tank full of piranhas. So do you want to come clean with me now?" he asked. "According to Louie Pelfrey, you are your own little mob. When I asked about you, he told me to stay as far away from you as possible," Jax said, following me close behind.

"That's because I have a little bit of a past." I used my finger and thumb to create a little space between them. My finger looked good on my hand. I liked my fingers. All of them. I couldn't scrape the image of a bunch of sharp fish teeth chomping on it.

"A little? Should I refresh your memory? Conned a preacher. Classic." He paused and pointed at the Walnut Grove Savings behind us. "Stole money from the bank. Federal offense. That is enough for me to arrest you right here." His voice escalated as he read off the past I had been working hard to forget from his little notebook. "Listen, Laurel. Trigger Finger Tony eats girls like you as a snack. He wouldn't hesitate to put a bullet through that pretty little head of yours and out of your gorgeous eyes. It wouldn't cross his mind a second time if he killed you. One wrong move and you're dead. Understand? Dead!"

"You don't know a thing about me. I've been working really hard to be on the level." I made it around the bank and stomped up the steps, even though he called me pretty and referred to my eyes as gorgeous.

“Oh, and are we back to robbing the bank tonight?” He continued to climb with me.

“If you were really with the FBI, you’d know I live here numb nuts.” I got my keys out of my bag and opened the door. Henrietta ran under the couch.

“Nice. Real mature, Laurel.” He stopped at the door and put a hand on each side, leaning into the efficiency. “So are you going to let me in?”

“No!” I slammed the door in his face, not caring a bit if I chopped off a finger or two.

## Chapter Nine

There wasn't a need for me to set my alarm. My mind kept me up all night wondering if everything Jax had said was true. The FBI part, not my past. Hell, everyone in Walnut Grove groaned when they heard my name and would be more than happy to tell anyone that would listen about my past. I had become sort of like an Urban Legend around here. Flattering at times, but not this time.

After dumping Henrietta a can of food in her bowl, I decided it was time to get ready and face the man Jax called Trigger Finger Tony.

I threw the skinny jeans from last night on because they weren't dirty and laundry wasn't at the top of my list these days since I had to go to Trixie's to wash and fold, plus I wasn't good at it. I found a blue sweater and sneakers to throw on before I headed out the door.

"Morning, Laurel." Sally Bent had parked her car next to the Old Girl in the back of the bank parking lot. She was a teller and took every advantage to tell me she had a real job. "I heard you got a new car and that you just might have a new job. Sorry about Morty."

I couldn't swear to it, but I think there was a twinkle of pleasure in her eyes. I knew she was referring to the prostituting thing Louie was spreading around.

"Tell your brother to keep his mouth shut," I said through my gritted teeth. "Because if he doesn't," I paused. "Well, you don't want to know what Laurel London has up her sleeve."

Rarely did I refer to myself in third person but it seemed to have more of an effect when I did. Besides, scaring Sally Bent was one pleasure I did have at the orphanage after she would run and tattle on everyone.

"I don't know who you think you are, but you can't go around threatening people all of your life." Sally walked fast toward the bank, clutching her fancy high dollar hand bag to her chest like I was going to rob her or something. "Grow up, Laurel London! You aren't at the orphanage anymore standing behind Trixie. You could get into real trouble threatening people."

"I think you have forgotten who saved your ass from that horrid Foster-Scissorhands!" I screamed, reminding her how she had been sent to a foster home where the mom had cut Sally's long black hair so short, you couldn't tell if she was a Sal or Sally.

It was the most pitiful thing I had seen when we saw her on our weekly Salvation Army donation dump in the parking lot behind the Dollar Store. Sally couldn't bring herself to look at us. She was miserable and I could see it in her eyes. I took matters into my own hands when Trixie wouldn't and kidnapped Sally in the middle of the night, bringing her back to the orphanage.

Trixie didn't have the heart to send her back. Shortly after that was when the Pelfreys adopted her.

"That was years ago!" she screamed back, flinging that long horse's mane over her shoulders like she was somehow better than me. Her hair was so long, I put money on it that she hadn't had it cut since.

If she hadn't disappeared into the bank and if I wasn't banned from going in there, I would have knocked her out.

"Bitch," I murmured and got into the car. My mind was full of questions for Trigger Finger Tony, if he was even who Jax Jackson claimed the guy to be.

I had tucked the money in my bag so I could give it back to him. If he was Trigger Finger Tony, I didn't want my fingerprints on any illegal crap. Though the money would come in real handy until I found a job.

"The Underworld Music Festival my ass." I pulled out of the lot and headed south on Second Street before I took a left and parked in front of The Cracked Egg. I had to grab a cup of coffee before I did anything.

It made more sense than ever how Jax Jackson asked me all of those questions about the festival and the note I had dropped off in New York. He didn't have any of those answers. He must've seen Trigger get out of my car and put two-and-two together. He was good.

"Morning!" Gia screamed over the counter. The breakfast crowd was there in full force.

I nodded a few hellos as I made my way to the counter.

"So," Gia chomped on her gum. She stuck the pen from her hand into her bun. "Did you get a good night kiss from Mr. New York City?"

"A…no," I said with my mouth and eyes wide open. I took a couple dollars out of my bag. "I need a large coffee to go." I laid the cash on the counter.

"I don't want your money." Gia pushed money back toward me. "I want you to dish. Why don't you come over for dinner tonight? Carmine is working late. You know…," she leaned over the counter. Her hair smelled like I had stepped into Bath and Body Works. Gia stocked up on all that lotion and stuff whenever she went shopping in Louisville, even though she had a closet full and could open up her own Bath and Body store. "Carmine said he has never seen Jax Jackson at Porty Morty's. In fact, the only one Morty has been dealing with was the woman with the chopsticks in her hair."

"Did he know her name?" I asked in case I did decide to tell Jax about her. It seemed like a good lead.

She shook her head. "Dinner?" she asked again.

There was a lot I wanted to ask her about this chopstick lady and a lot I had to tell her but The Cracked Egg wasn't the place. "Yea, dinner sounds great. I've got something to tell you about Jax Jackson." I grabbed my cup of coffee.

"Oh! I can't wait." Gia rubbed her hands together before she waved me off. "See you later." I watched her grab the coffee pot and fill all the customers' cups lined up down the counter with a big smile on her face before I left.

My mind was rolling around all sorts of crazy situations about the woman with the chopsticks and how she could or couldn't be related to the whole Trigger thing. I kept telling myself it wasn't my place to figure it out, but I couldn't help myself.

My mind was going as fast as I was driving the car. Mob? What was the mob doing in Walnut Grove? What was there that they wanted? Trust me, I had been all over that town, legally and illegally, there was nothing there. Did Trigger and chopstick girl have something to do with each other?

Trigger Finger Tony was standing outside of the Airport Hotel waiting.

"I knew I could count on you." He was dressed a little more suitable to be the mob guy he was supposed to be in his three-piece white suit. The gold chains dripped around his neck made my mob radar go way up and all my questions out the window. My mind was numb.

Not that I ever had a mob radar, but there were plenty of times I had watched shows like "Married to the Mob" and "Mob Wives" to know a little bit about their lives. There were times I had dreamed of being as powerful as a mob boss, but I never wanted to actually be associated with a mob boss.

"What?" He got in the back and slammed the door. "You still mad about the phone thing?"

I didn't say a word. I put the car in drive and headed back toward Walnut Grove. I wasn't sure what to say.

"Come on, I don't feel bad about doing it," he scoffed.

I glanced at him in the rearview mirror. He stared back with blank animal eyes. I focused back on the road.

"Besides, I gave you enough cash to get you a real phone, not the dollar store junk you had." He opened his suit coat.

I gripped the steering wheel tightly with both hands to keep them from shaking. A knot settled in my throat. I swallowed hard to get it down, but the knot didn't budge. I didn't know how to start the conversation that I was going to give him back his mob money and never pick him up again.

"I'm packing too!" I yelled and winced when he pulled his hand out, knowing he was going to shoot me.

My eyes felt like they had exploded open when I saw he didn't have his creepy black gloves on and it exposed his hand minus a pointer finger.

"Eeck!" I threw my hand over my mouth and tried to steadily drive with the other one. Trigger Finger Tony, Jax Jackson's voice played over and over in my head. I put my hand back on the wheel and looked at my two pointer fingers.

They suited me nicely and I was not planning on losing them anytime soon.

"Packing." He chuckled.

Damn. He wasn't a bit scared by my little friend. In fact, his reaction scared me.

"I hope you haven't spent all the money I gave you yesterday." He licked his thumb and started to count out more money from the wad of cash in his other hand. "You seem to be able to keep your mouth shut, so I think I'm going to have to ask you to take a leave of absence from your job and just be my personal driver while I'm in town."

"I'm not that trustworthy." Shit, shit, shit. How was I going to get myself out of this one? If I took the money, Jax would be right. I would be working for the mob if Trigger was a mob man. "I mean," God, I was going to get myself shot. Or worse…my finger eaten by a fish! "I mean…," I hesitated.

"Is there a problem with the money?" He pulled a few more bills from his stack. "Fine. I'll give you more." He tossed the entire stack of hundreds over the front seat. They scattered all over the passenger side. "I'm trusting you can drop me off at the docks in Walnut Grove and bring me back tonight around five."

Without hesitation or thinking about my actions, my mouth opened wide, real wide, "At your service."

Crap! Not being able to resist the thrill of something going down had never been a good trait of mine and those situations always turned out bad. This was a bad situation.

"I mean, I can't. I really wish I could, but—" I tried to continue, but Trigger Finger Tony interrupted me.

"What is your name?" he asked.

"Laurel." One word answers, stick with one word answers, I told myself. Stand your ground.

"Laurel what, honey?" His hand, minus a finger, dangled over the seat. His chunky middle finger had no problem making up for his missing pointer as it was nice and snug in the trigger guard of a pistol dangling off of it. "You have to have a last name. Me and my little friend would like to know what it is."

"London. Laurel London." To hell with one word answers. I had to save my life.

"Well, Laurel London. I hope we don't find ourselves at a crossroads of misunderstanding. You see," he leaned back and brought the gun up to his lips. He made sure I was looking at him in the rearview before he kissed it. "When I put my mind to something, I don't change it. No one, not even Laurel London can change it or tell me no. Capisce?"

"I'm not sure who you think you are, but I have a life outside of you as a customer." My voice cracked.

I swallowed hard before I glanced back in the rearview mirror and quickly turned my head back to the front as he was glaring at me. No smile. Dead stare.

My head started to ache and my stomach rolled like I had to use the bathroom. Instantly I had to wonder if I had some sort of disease. Maybe that Irritable Bowl Syndrome or something. Was that a hereditary disease? Or was it just the stress of my crazy life?

Stress of losing a job. Stress of Jax Jackson. Stress of losing a finger. Stress of possibly having a mob boss in my car.

"Do you like the money Laurel?" he asked.

"Yes, but I don't like your little friend. It makes me nervous and a little stressed out." There was no reason to lie to him; I knew I was going to have to do what he said because everything Jax had said to me about Trigger Finger Tony played over in my head like a movie. I never planned on being anyone's snack. "I think it made me stressed out because I have this stomach thing. Though it could be a hereditary thing and I just don't know about it because..."

"Because you were an orphan," Trigger finished my sentence in a snide sort of way. "Yeah, yeah. Enough of that bullshit. What about the money?"

"I don't know who you are, but if you acted like a regular taxi passenger without a gun, maybe I wouldn't be so taken aback by your very generous offer."

"Okay little darlin'. Let's say I put my friend away and we go legit by me hiring you to be my driver for as long as I need you. We have these services in New York that will come and pick you up and drop you off. No questions asked." Trigger Finger Tony made a good offer. "I pay you under the table and you don't report a thing to the IRS. Or cops."

"And you aren't going to hurt me?" I gulped. I had never really thought about my fingers, but now that I took a closer look I was becoming a little partial to them. I turned down River Road. I couldn't get to the docks fast enough.

"Hurt you?" Trigger Finger Tony laughed. "Why would I hurt you?" His eyes lowered. "See you around five." He held up his hand. "Get a phone."

"Is that really four? Or is that five?" My smart comment shot out of my mouth before I could stop it.

A tilted grin flipped up in the left corner of his lip. "Five." He flipped me a few more Benjamins before he got out of the car.

"Damn, damn, damn!" I beat the steering wheel with the palm of my hand.

Guilt dropped in my gut like a bowling ball. By order of Jax Jackson and for my safety, I was supposed to drop him off and tell him I couldn't do any more driving. But no…I let the money entice me right back into Anthony Cardozza's inner circle of bad. Whatever that was.

I eased back out on River Road and head back to town. I had to get a strong cup of coffee and an appointment with the doctor. I held my hand up. It was shaking like a leaf. My stomach hurt so much that I felt like I needed to lie down. There wasn't a time that I could recall me ever feeling this way.

"Cool as a cucumber, Laurel London. You are tough. Tough. Shit!" I screamed when I swerved off the road and into a ditch trying to avoid a man.

I gripped the wheel and took a few deep breaths to make sure I was still alive and that I hadn't just crapped myself.

"Are you okay?" Jax Jackson stood at my window and gestured for me to roll it down when he couldn't open the locked driver's side door.

"I'm fine." I got out, a little shaky, but my stomach wasn't hurting. "What the hell were you doing in the middle of the road?"

"I've been staking out the docks. I have to walk since there isn't a cab around here. A real cab company." Jax clenched his fists. "Didn't you see me from way back there?" He uncurled his hands and pointed behind us. "I saw your big yellow car coming. That is why I was flagging you down."

He walked out of the ditch and into the middle of the country road; there was a stalking, purposeful intent in his walk.

"I didn't see you until it was almost too late." I shook my head.

"Now you're screwing with me. I think you were trying to hit me." Jax turned toward me. His eyes watched me with a renewed interest. "Were you?"

"No. I'm…," I flung my hands in the air. "I'm stressed. I swear I am." I busted out in tears. Ever since meeting Trigger and Jax, my life had been turned upside down, right side up and back twisted. "I bet I have an ulcer. I need to get to the doctor."

"I'm so sorry Laurel." He brought me to him and nestled me into his arms. "I can't let you do this anymore."

What? Do what? Hug on me? Because I had to admit it felt really good.

He pulled me away from him at arm's length. Silently I studied him and he studied me back. His gaze moved, traveling up and down me. I could almost feel his thoughts.

"Do what?" I finally asked, breaking the silence.

"We are going to have to work together." He dropped his hands to his side and ran his fingers through his hair, something I thoroughly wanted to do. "You are going to have to be on the mob payroll and FBI payroll."

"Whoa!" I backed up toward my car by walking backward. "I'm not on anyone's payroll. I might be a good con here in little ole Walnut Grove, but I'm not enough of a con to help any sort of mob shit taking place in Walnut Grove. I'll tuck my tail between my legs and go beg for a job at the bank if I need money that bad."

"It's not about money. It's about doing what I need to do to bring down Trigger Finger Tony Cardozza. That includes you." He pointed a finger at me. "For some reason he likes you and the FBI needs to use it to our advantage."

"I don't know about any of this." I wrapped my arms around my stomach when the pain suddenly appeared. I for sure had some sort of whacky disease and it was vital I found out my family history.

Jax continued to walk toward me.

The closer he got, the faster I walked backward until I stepped off the road into the grassy brush a little behind my car and fell flat on my ass.

"Damn!" I jumped up, my feet in the messy marsh. "The county needs to get out here and mow this grass." I looked down and pulled my foot up. The grass was smashed where I had stepped. There was a finger that was stuck straight up in the mud. "Oh shit! Shit! Shit!" I jumped out of the marsh grass and back out on the road.

"What?" Jax rushed over. He took his small pad of paper out of his pocket and got the pencil out of the spiral. He used the pencil tip to push the finger out of the mud. "Oh God. Trigger strikes again."

"What does that mean?" I begged to know. My insides felt like they were having their own little carnival inside. I felt like I was about to blow chunks any minute.

"The ring looks like one of his guys. Nicoli Fabrizo." He used his foot to lightly brush the top of the grass. "No body. Probably sending Nicoli a message."

"Message?"

"That's what he does. Takes a finger here and there to make sure his people don't stray. Nicoli probably did something that didn't set well with him and he taught him a lesson."

"So he isn't dead?" I asked. Missing a finger and alive was a much better situation than missing a finger and dead.

"I'd say he is alive, but in a little pain." Jax looked around the grassy area. "Enough pain that he will remember not to cross Trigger again."

"This Nicoli is here too?" Shivers traveled up my body. There was an intense feeling that I had gotten myself into something much deeper than I could handle.

"Has to be. The ring has a big N printed on it and the insignia is the Cardozza family crest." He ripped a piece of paper out of his notepad and reached down. He grabbed the finger. "See." He held up the dark, dried up bloody digit for me to see.

"There went my appetite." I had to look away in fear I was going to throw up right there. "What about these rings?"

"There isn't really any significance to them. Only that each employee of Trigger's has one. It's kind of like a status thing." He shrugged and began to elaborate, "When one of Trigger's men walk into a bar or restaurant in Jersey or the city, everyone knows not to mess with them—that he's part of the Cardozza cartel, mob, whatever you want to call it."

"That makes sense." I studied the ring a little closer to get a better look in case I did happen to see anyone around Walnut Grove wearing one. "Do we need to call the police?"

"I am the police. The FBI." He shook his head and folded the finger in the paper. "I'll make sure I get this back to the Louisville lab for evidence. That is why I'm not touching it."

"For prints or something?" I asked trying to pretend I knew what it was all about.

"Something like that." He grinned. "You okay?"

“No. No. I’m definitely not okay.” I tried to shake it off, but burst out in tears. “I’m really not tough.”

“You are tough.” He walked back over and tried to embrace me again which would have been great if the finger wasn’t in his grip. “Oh. Sorry.”

“I’m fine. Really.” Now was the time to get on my big girl pants. “I think we should tell Derek about this.”

“Bowling Derek?”

“He’s my friend and he is in the training program at the University of Louisville to become a police officer,” I said with full confidence that Derek would know what to do.

I put my hand on the outside door handle of the car to open the door. I was going to take myself directly to Derek’s garage and get all this stress off of me.

“That is not going to happen.” Jax planted his hand on the door jam, not allowing me to open it even though I gave it a few quick tugs. “This is an FBI investigation. It’s completely on the down low. If anyone finds out about this in the public, all residents of Walnut Grove are in danger. Do you want that on you too?”

“Umm…no,” meekly I answered. “I’ve been trying to get on the level around here.”

"Then help us out. The FBI." His words "help us out" did have a nice ring to it. "Only you can't tell anyone. Not even Derek or the local police."

"You will keep me safe?" I asked. "Will you keep Trixie safe?"

"If you cooperate and do what I ask you to do. Not go off on some rampage of your own and get all hot headed where we both will be in danger," he paused. "Who is Trixie?"

"She is my guardian." I bit the side of my lip wondering if I should tell him my story.

"Guardian?"

"I grew up in an orphanage." I paused to gather my thoughts because I wasn't sure how much I wanted him to know. Then it hit me. "Oh, but I bet you knew that already and that Trixie was the head of it. She still thinks she has to take care of me."

"Um…," he hesitated and looked at his little notebook. "Yes, I knew about that. And we can keep you both safe."

Hearing him say that made me feel a tad bit better. Not a whole lot. But a little.

There were two things I liked about this whole idea. One, having to be around Jax sounded great. And two…well I really couldn't think of another, but my one reason was good enough for me.

"Deal. On one more condition." I put my hand out for him to shake. "You don't keep me in the dark."

"Not if you cooperate." His hand curled around mine. He gripped it…tight. Slowly we shook on it, but deep in my gut I knew he wasn't telling me the full truth.

## Chapter Ten

After I took Jax back to the Windmill and gave Louie the old I'm watching you gesture, I went home and took a long, very long nap with Henrietta curled up on my pillow next to me. My head was hurting from all the stuff Jax had told me, Trigger Finger Tony, and the idea that I could possibly have some sort of family disease didn't make me feel better.

I had also grabbed the cash out of Henrietta's litter box. I counted out over five thousand dollars that Trigger had given me. I put five hundred in my bag. The rest wasn't going to fit in Henrietta's shit box so I put the money in a couple baggies and taped them on the inside of the return air vent in the bathroom. Not that someone was going to break in and steal from me, but I was always careful.

"Let's go." I grabbed Henrietta's leash when I noticed it was almost five o'clock. "Time to pick up Trigger."

Henrietta stretched out and opened her mouth into a yawn before she sauntered over to the door.

She liked to go outside and sit on the steps and sunbathe. I always put a leash on her so she wouldn't dart off after a bird or something. But deep down, I didn't want to take the chance of losing her. A fear I had. It seemed like I held on to dear life to all the people in my life in fear of them walking away from me. Then on the opposite side, I made sure I had a hard heart so I wouldn't get hurt.

"We are going for a ride and then to Gia's." I clipped the leash on her before I opened the door and walked down the steps to the car.

Henrietta was used to riding in the car. I took her on a lot of client calls when I worked at Porty Morty's. I enjoyed her company. She loved Gia. Since I had been gone all day, I couldn't bear to leave her alone for the next few hours.

"What the hell is that?" Trigger snarled at Henrietta.

She had found a nice warm spot on the long dashboard of the Old Girl and curled up. I had a deep-set pang of envy when Henrietta barely squeaked open her eyes to get a look at the mobster. She didn't have time for him. I wish I had felt the same and could have walked away.

"That's the cab company's mascot. Henrietta," I lied, but it sounded good.

If I couldn't find a job, I guessed I could open a taxi business. After all there wasn't one in Walnut Grove. Kitty Kab, Cat Cab, all sorts of names formed in my head.

"Keep it away from me." He curled his thick nose, making his cheeks fatter than they already were. "I can't stand cats. Don't trust them."

"Feeling is mutual," I muttered.

Trigger was unusually silent for most of the trip. He clicked away on his phone like he was texting someone. A few times Henrietta popped her head up and looked directly back at him as if she was keeping her eye on him too.

Trigger let out a few groans and snarls during his ride, but he never said a word until he got out at the Airport Hotel and gave me instructions to pick him up at nine a.m. the next morning.

I agreed only because that was part of my job as a newly employed undercover agent for the FBI.

As soon as Trigger had gotten out of the car, Henrietta got up and jumped down onto the passenger seat with her paws on the door. She loved putting her nose out the window, so I reached over and rolled down the window before we headed back to Walnut Grove to Gia's house.

I was starving. And I couldn't wait to tell her about my new job.

"It's about time you got here." Gia stood in the doorway on her small stoop with her hands on her hips. "I've been calling your phone and it's dead."

"Literally," I grumbled under my breath and clipped on Henrietta's leash.

"Do you think I come from a line of crazies?" I asked when Henrietta and I walked up to her house.

"What do you mean?" she asked and picked up Henrietta.

Immediately Henrietta purred because she knew Gia was going to give her a good ear itching.

I followed them into the small ranch her father had given her when she got married to Carmine. He even had a fancy interior decorator come down from Louisville to help her make it exactly like Gia wanted.

She was modern to the core. All leather furniture, even leather kitchen chairs, stainless steel appliances and countertops, fancy Italian stoves (two) and bamboo flooring. Her walls were all sorts of color blocked brights from yellows to black. Gia, hands down, had the best decorated house in Walnut Grove.

We plopped down on her couch in the combo kitchen and family room. I pulled the orange bolster pillow into my lap and hugged it. Henrietta darted off to find the cat scratch stand Gia kept there just for her.

"You know where you come from." I bit my lip. "I don't. What if my parents were some sort of loons and I become some sort of loon?"

It was a valid question.

"What are you talking about?" The lines between Gia's brows creased.

"I have this stomach thing. I wonder if I have an ulcer or something worse." I pushed on my gut.

"Have you asked Trixie? I bet she knows something." Gia shrugged. She sat down and reached over and put her hand on my leg.

"No. She always acts so offended when I ask her. Like she didn't take good care of me, when she did." I inhaled deeply before I let out a big worry sigh. "And she says I'm a hypochondriac with nothing to worry about."

"Why are you worried? Is it the stress of losing your job?"

"No. Well, maybe since I am working undercover for the FBI." I tried to contain my smile.

It was so cool to even think I was undercover.

"Okay. You might be a little stressed." Gia didn't seem as excited as me. She stood up and reached for the cordless phone on the coffee table. "I'm going to call my mom and see if she can get you into her psychiatrist like tomorrow."

I jumped up and grabbed the phone out of her hands.

"You can't do that! You can't tell anyone. You are sworn to secrecy." I held onto the phone for dear life.

"We aren't in sixth grade, Laurel. You seriously need some help." Gia took a deep breath. "Okay." She sat back down and patted the couch for me to sit. "Why do you think you are working for the FBI?"

"Jax Jackson. He really isn't here on business with the Underworld Music Festival. In fact, he didn't even know about the festival until I spilled my guts to him the day I first drove him to the Windmill. He is here because they are keeping tabs on Trigger Finger Tony Cardozza."

"What is the mob doing in Walnut Grove?" Gia asked.

"I don't know. The FBI doesn't seem to know." My brows rose. "They just know that wherever he goes, trouble follows and he's good at covering his tracks. But he gets dropped off at the docks and picked up by me every single day. Which makes me think that if someone is going to

Porty Morty's about the Underworld Music Festival, maybe Trigger has something to do with it."

"What did Jax think about that?" Gia was getting all into it. I could see her wheels turning up in her head.

"We haven't discussed it. He is all secretive and stuff." I leaned back on the couch. "We are meeting up tomorrow to discuss what all the FBI wants me to do."

"Oh God, Laurel." Deep worry settled in Gia's big brown eyes. "You can't go putting yourself in danger."

"He promised I wouldn't be in any danger."

Gia snapped her fingers. "Carmine said chopstick girl was there again today. When I told him to investigate the music festival, he said that there wasn't anything on the account. I mean nothing on any accounts." Her brows rose in curiosity. "Do you think chopstick girl could be part of all of this Trigger stuff?"

"I don't know, but it's a good question to look into." I made a mental note to tell Jax.

"Carmine said that he thinks Morty is having money problems."

"Money problems?" That didn't make sense. Morty had had a ton of events on the books before I had left. "That's too bad."

"So back to Jax and this crazy FBI idea," Gia coaxed me along.

I went ahead and told her everything from the cash, Trigger Finger Tony and the real finger I had tripped over in the tall grass on River Road.

Her face contorted all around along with a big long, "Ewww."

"I know," I agreed.

"Let's see if any of this is on Google." Gia went to the stove where she took the casserole out of the oven. "Chicken and rice. You'll love it. While it cools, we can search the Internet."

She turned the oven off and opened the laptop that was sitting on her kitchen table. She pushed it toward me.

"Go on. Search."

"Anthony Cardozza." I typed in his name and hit send.

"Jesus, Laurel. There are thirty pages of Google on him." She reached around and used her long fingernail to move the mouse to the images button.

It didn't take any time for a page full of Trigger Finger Tony to pop up, staring right back at us. The crooked grin in most of them. There were some pictures of him in floor length fur coats, stacks of jewelry, and women dripping off him.

"That's him," I confirmed. "The ring." I pointed to all the pictures. "Every single person surrounding him has the same ring. Just like Jax said."

"Who is she?" Gia pointed to the scantly-clad woman who dripped off Trigger like his gold necklaces.

"I don't know. He just pays me to drive him back and forth from the docks to the Airport Hotel. We don't talk personal life stuff. Really we didn't talk at all tonight. He just told me to pick him up at nine a.m. tomorrow."

I went back to the Google search screen and typed in Jax Jackson.

"There's nothing here." My eyes scanned down the screen. I put my finger at the top one and went down. "Surely I missed something."

"Hmm. Click the images." Gia pointed to the image search.

I clicked.

A ton of pictures turned up but none of them stood out as him.

"He doesn't look like any of these people. Do you think he's lying to you?" Gia asked a good question, putting a little doubt in my head. "You know I have a really good bullshit meter. And I have to say it dinged a little when I was around him at the bowling alley."

"Well, he has been really secretive. He knew who Trigger was. He also didn't want me to call Derek when I tripped on the finger." I stared at a picture of a funeral on the screen.

All the men, dressed in black, were carrying a casket down the steps of what looked like an old church. I leaned down and looked closer.

"I need to make this one bigger," I said.

"Click on it," Gia said acting like I didn't know my way around a laptop.

"Duh. I've been hacking computers a long time now. I know what I'm doing. Remember?" I reminded Gia of how we first met the day at the library. She was trying to check out a book but the librarian said she had to bring the others back first. Gia was so sad and cried. I followed her out of the library and told her that I could break into the library computer and wipe her library card clean. Of course she agreed. End of story.

"Shoot me." She put her hands in the air. "You said you were going on the straight and narrow. And this." She made a circular motion with her finger at the computer. "This is definitely not the straight and narrow."

I clicked on the picture again which took me to the website where the picture was originally posted. It was the obituaries in The New York Times.

The accompanying article read:

> Federal Bureau of Investigation officer Lance McAllister was gunned down during a raid with known mobster Anthony "Trigger Finger Tony" Cardozza. In attendance at his funeral were other FBI agents, including McAllister's long-time partner Jax Jackson.

"Here!" I tapped my nail on the screen. "It says here that he's an FBI agent and that his partner was killed in the line of duty. The FBI believed that Trigger Finger Tony Cardozza's cartel was behind the hit." I held my hand up in the air with my pointer finger tucked under. "Oh God, Gia. He is undercover. I'm freaking working for the FBI and the mob!"

Gia squealed so loud, Henrietta darted through the kitchen and down the hall.

"This is so awesome! I'm so jealous!" She jumped up and down. "This means you need a gun."

"Gun?" That was something I so did not need.

"You have to protect yourself. Even if you don't load it, you got to have it to wave around if something goes wrong." She cocked her brows and twerked her head back and forth.

She was right. I would be a real badass if I carried a gun. Not that it would be loaded or anything, but if Trigger tried to pull something funny, I might be able to scare him with it.

Gia leaned back over the laptop and looked at the article.

"I hope he has your back." Concern dripped out of her mouth.

"He said he was going to protect me."

"Just like he had his dead partner's back? About that gun." Gia had me there. She knew exactly the right buttons to push. "Since you have a little bit of cash to spend," she eyed me suspiciously, "we can look on Craigslist."

"Fine." The idea didn't set well with me, but I knew it was something I had to do. I was in no situation to be without protection.

I typed in "hand guns" on Craigslist and a slew of them popped up.

"That's cute." Gia's eyes twinkled. "Oh God! Laurel, you are so lucky!"

I sent the seller a quick email and made sure I told them I could only respond to emails.

"Remind me again how I'm lucky?" I couldn't wait to hear what she had to say. Just a few short minutes ago I was ready to check myself into a behavioral health facility.

"You get to go undercover with a cool gun and hot guy while I get to stay around The Cracked Egg and watch Louie Pelfrey gorge himself." She smiled.

We busted out into laughter. That was one of the special things we did and I loved it. Gia was more of a sister than a friend. I wondered if I had a real sister. Hell, I'd even take a stinky brother for that matter.

"What?" She stopped laughing and looked at me.

"What?" I asked.

"All of the sudden you got a serious look."

"Oh," I blew her off. I didn't want to get into the whole pity-poor-orphan-Annie act. I had accepted my fate a long time ago. I could do the research without telling anyone, that way, if I came up on the wrong trail, I didn't have to bother explaining it all. "I wonder what Trigger is doing down at the docks. And if Morty has anything to do with it."

"I don't know, but I'm telling Carmine to be careful." Gia drummed her fingers together.

"No. You can't tell Carmine anything. I told you it was top secret." I pretended to lock my lips like kids did when they were sworn to secrecy. "You agreed."

"Okay. But promise me you won't let yourself get into trouble."

"Promise. Let's eat. I'm starving."

In reality I wasn't a bit hungry. In fact, since these whole crazy new twists of events after Morty fired me, I hadn't had an appetite.

## Chapter Eleven

After dinner I checked my email from Gia's computer. The Craigslist gun owner emailed back and told me to meet near the docks at nine thirty p.m. It was just enough time to go check on Trixie and try to get a few questions answered about my past.

The stress of the situation I had gotten myself into had made me feel crazy and sick to my stomach which made me believe it was in my genes. Trixie had to know something. She knew something about every other kid in the orphanage. Maybe not who their parents were, but she knew where some of them were born and other little things. With my skills, I'd be able to take a small lead and find something, anything.

Trixie's house wasn't too far from the docks.

She had always wanted a little vegetable garden and chicken coup for fresh eggs, so she bought the little two-bedroom cottage on River Road with enough land to have everything she wanted.

It was a nice out which meant she was doing one of two things. Either sitting on the porch with her nightly cocktail or weeding out her garden.

Luckily for me, it was the first.

“What is your pleasure or pain?” She held up the clear glass with nothing but ice in it. She wiggled the cup causing the ice to jingle against the sides.

“What do you have? Or did you have?” I snickered. Trixie was known to tip back a time or two. Henrietta used the full extension on her leash to smell around and roll around in something I was sure was some sort of chicken poop.

“Vodka on the rocks. Good for the spirit.” She winked. She got out of the rocker and made it over to the door. Her hair was still covered by her foil hat. She had on a denim mini-skirt and a jersey-styled top with the number twenty-nine printed on the front. The ice stopped clinking together but the bracelets that lined her wrist jingled.

“If you are sure you aren’t expecting company.” Trixie was far too dressed up to just be home alone. Most nights she laid around in her leopard print bathrobe and fuzzy slippers. “I’ll take what you have.”

"You never know who might pop over." She flung the screen door open and disappeared.

The door slammed shut. Sounded just like a gunshot, nearly knocking me out of the chair. I was still so jumpy from all the turn of events from the last two days, I had no idea how I was keeping it together.

A few minutes later she was kicking the door open with her foot and handing me the ever-so-needed drink. Maybe this was all I needed for the stress.

"Cheers!" We clinked glasses.

My skin nearly melted off my body because she'd made the drink so strong.

"So," Trixie eased herself back into her rocker. Her eyes on me. "What is wrong with your phone?"

"I think it's broken." I took another drink to avoid eye contact.

"Really? Because when I pinged it, it says that you are on River Road." She leaned on the arm of the rocker with her elbow, hand and glass in the air, with her pinky finger out. "I gave Clyde the coordinates and he said it was in a ditch somewhere. Do you know that I thought you were in a ditch? Dead."

"Well I'm not." I smiled and took another drink. Her coolness was evidence that she wasn't approving of my responses to her questions.

"I know. Derek said he saw your big yellow car around town. So then I knew you were alive."

"You have it set up so I'm pingable?" I wasn't sure if pingable was a word, but it seemed to fit her crime.

"I like keeping tabs on you." Trixie chugged the last of her drink and let out a big sigh. "Especially now, since there seems to be some funny business going on."

"There is no funny business going on."

Unless you wanted to count a mob boss giving me loads of cash to drive him around and the FBI asking me to be on their payroll to help bring down the aforementioned mob boss.

"Which reminds me." I sucked in a big breath. "Do you know anything about my parents?"

She shook her head, staring straight ahead.

"Nothing? Not even where I come from?" I stuck my finger in my drink and twirled it around to try to mix it a little better or even hope the ice cubes would help water it down.

"Why you come from right here. Walnut Grove, Kentucky." She didn't look at me.

"You mean my parents were from here?" That couldn't be right. Everyone was in everyone's business and I would have heard some sort of tale if that was the case.

"Nope. You've been with me since you were a day old. I didn't ask questions. Not my part." She used the heels of her feet to slowly rock her chair back and forth. "You were cute. Did I ever tell you about the time—"

"Stop right there," I interrupted. "Every single time I ask you about my past, you always want to tell me a story starting with 'did I tell you' and I need to know."

"I don't know." She shrugged. I noted she never looked at me once. "All I know was that there was a note attached to you that said to take good care of you. I've done that, haven't I?"

"Yes," I said with quiet emphasis. That wasn't enough to stop me. "Do you have the note?"

She shook her head back and forth.

"Where are my records?" There had to be records. I remember the orphanage office was filled to the gills with records.

"You didn't come with any. Found you in a box on my steps with the note."

"Yes. I know that. But didn't you tell the police?" I asked. I mean it wasn't like it was ancient times and I had floated down the river like Moses or something.

"Of course they knew. But Walnut Grove Police Department wasn't going to waste time trying to find somebody who didn't want to be found." Her words hit a spot directly in the middle of my gut.

She was right. They didn't want to be found which meant they didn't want me.

"How is the job search? I was meaning to get down there and give Morty a piece of my mind."

"That's exactly why I wanted my background information. My mind. I need to know if anyone in my family had any diseases or say…mental health issues?"

"The only thing I bet was in your family was a long line of criminals after what you put me through." She gave me a sideways glance and laughed. "Now drink up."

No matter how much I tried, there was no way I was going to get it out of her. I was going to have to figure out where those records were. Surely there was something in the files about me.

Trixie and I didn't bring up my past again. We talked about jobs I could apply for. Most of them were in Louisville, which wasn't bad since it was only a thirty minute drive. I was getting used to it since I had become Trigger Finger's personal driver.

"Oh." Thinking about Tony jarred my memory of my meeting with the gun owner from Craigslist. "Got to get going if I'm going to drive to Louisville in the morning to look for a job."

Trixie got up.

"Let me get you some gas money." She held her hand on the metal handle of the screen door.

"I'm good. I'm still using the little bit of guilt money Morty gave me." I lied, but she didn't need to know anything about Tony, the mob, Jax Jackson or the finger. She would have a heart attack for sure and die. Then I'd really be gone.

I smiled at her. Her face softened into a sweet grin. She really was all I needed, but it sure would be nice just to know my DNA.

"I thought you said you were going to pay Pastor Wilson and Rita upfront rent money," she questioned me.

"I did. But it didn't take all my money," I lied again…

"I'll talk to you tomorrow," Trixie said. She was a little leery. I leaned over and we hugged. "I don't know what happened to your phone, but go get another one." She shook her finger at me. "Do you understand?"

"Yes. I will." I grabbed Henrietta and we jumped back into the Belvedere and headed east toward the docks.

I eased the Old Girl right next to Morty's. It was well lit there… most of the time. The dock light looked like it needed to be replaced.

The sound of a boat knocking up against the dock caused me to look down at Morty's dock because there were flashlights wiggling all around. Two of them to be exact.

I ducked behind the old dumpster and held my nose.

"Let's get out of here!" I heard one of them say and the flashlights got closer as they seemed to dart up the ramp.

I kept myself hidden until they passed. It was probably a teenage couple, no doubt trying to get it on.

I came out from behind the dumpster and all of the sudden the dock light came on.

I saw a man on the dock. He lifted his head; his eyes locked with mine.

"Laurel, what are you doing down here?"

I jumped around. Derek was standing next to my car.

"I'm going to have to call Stanley Clever. He needs to get back out here and change these bulbs." Derek walked toward me, using his flashlight to guide his steps. He held a small silver case in his other hand.

"What?" Confused, I looked back at the dock. The man was gone, the light was out. I gulped. I didn't have a choice. I knew I was going to have to break into the old orphanage and get my records. I was completely losing my mind. "That was just on." My mouth fell open and I pointed to the dock.

"Not recently. Pastor Wilson had called the station and left a message a couple days ago." He shined the light in my eyes. I shielded it with my hand. "Sorry."

"No problem." Pastor Wilson? Hmm. That was the second time in the past couple of days he had been there. Why? What business did Friendship Baptist have to do with Morty? I shook it out of my head. "What are you doing down here?"

"I asked you first," Derek said in a joking manner. Only he didn't have a joking poker face.

It was a "thing" with us. The one-upping thing.

"Just getting some air." I kicked the rocks with my shoe. Derek was always good at calling me out on my lies.

"Right." He tipped his head back, his eyes looking down on me. "The truth now."

"Fine. I'm here to buy a gunoffsomeoneonCraigslist," I slurred the last few words so fast to confuse him.

"Did you say gun?" He held the silver case in the air. "Like a Colt Defender?"

"Yes." We both froze when we realized he was the seller and I was the buyer.

"Are you…," his mouth dropped. "Hackensack?"

"Yeah." I hung my head. I knew exactly what was coming.

"Geez Laurel!" He wasn't pleased. "Why in the hell do you need a gun? I can't sell you this. I bet you don't even have the right permits to carry." He turned and walked back toward my car. "Is there a slew of robberies at the Quick Copy?"

"Quick Copy?" My nose turned up. What on earth was he talking about?

"You told me you were going to apply as a salesperson at the Quick Copy selling copiers. That doesn't require a gun." He was walking faster and faster.

“I haven’t applied yet. I need the gun.” I ran after him and grabbed his arm. His blue eyes flashed with outrage. My hand dropped. “I mean, don’t you want me to be safe when I’m driving these people around?”

“People?” he questioned. “What people? I thought you said one ride with that arrogant salesman.”

“Jax Jackson,” I muttered.

“Name fits him,” he shot back. “And if you feel threatened by him, then we need to get to the bottom of it. Now!”

“He isn’t a problem. But he did ask if I could take him back and forth places so he could get around. I don’t mind, but I think a little protection might be nice.” Sounded good to me.

“You don’t even know how to shoot a gun.” He made a good point.

“I don’t want to use it, just have it right there and pretend I do,” I said. “If someone sees a gun, they are on their best behavior.”

“Sounds like you know.” He eyed me suspiciously.

“Duh, TV.” Not that I was going to tell him about Trigger Finger Tony and his love of showing me his little friend.

"I'm not selling it to you." He plopped the case on the Old Girl and opened it. As he took it out, I saw one of the bullets fall out and roll under the car. He didn't notice and kept talking, "I'll let you borrow it for show. That's it, Laurel."

He took the gun out and opened the barrel. He held it up in the air with one hand, the flashlight in the other. "Empty." He rolled the barrel and slammed it back in before he handed it to me.

"Thanks." I knew I had to get that bullet. If I had one, I could go to the store and buy more just like it without Derek ever knowing. "By the way, you don't have any old cell phones you aren't using lying around do you?"

"I have a couple at the shop. You can swing by and grab one. Take it on over to Johnny Delgato's place. He can have it running for you in no time."

"Great." Hearing Johnny's name made me cringe. He was one of those hunky guys with shifty eyes and sly hands. He was always trying to cop a feel at our high school dances. He had opened up the Phone Shop, not an original name, after he came back from a two-year college with some sort of business degree.

He must've known what he was doing because the Phone Shop was always packed.

"Get on out of here," he warned and walked back toward the street. Before he rounded the corner, he yelled over his shoulder, "Stay away from Jax Jackson!"

"Will do." Ugh…if he only knew that I had to work for Jax and the FBI, not to mention the mob.

I crouched down and looked under the car. It was pitch black. I got up and looked in the car to see if there might be a flashlight in there but there was nothing. The light above the dumpster flickered, and then buzzed on.

I bent down to look under the car. The bullet was right there by my foot. I grabbed it and put it in my pocket before I got back into the car.

## Chapter Twelve

Call me a hypochondriac or just plain crazy, but the idea that there could be something, anything about my past in the old orphanage sat in my gut next to my ulcer or whatever had to be growing in my stomach. It had to be hereditary.

Henrietta wasn't in any rush to get home because she was curled up in the back seat of the car, eyes shut tight.

I backed the car out and turned it around to turn onto River Road so I could head out to the abandoned orphanage. Before I pulled out, someone smacked the back of the trunk. In my rearview window I could see it was the couple of kids I had seen on the docks.

"Can you give us a lift? We don't have any money and if I don't get back by curfew my dad is going to kill him." The young blonde pointed to the scrawny guy next to her.

"Get in." I sighed heavily. I remembered what it was like being young, only I didn't have a ride anywhere.

They jumped in and muttered a few "thank yous" and told me how to get to her house. It was in the trailer park a few miles away.

"If you don't start giving it up, you won't have to worry about a curfew because I'm dumping you." The guy grabbed the girl by the leg making her wince.

"I told you. I'm not ready for that." Tears hung on the edge of her lids. "But Tommy I love you."

I reached over and pulled the little gun next to me.

"Then give me a little. That's how you show me." He grabbed her and planted a big kiss on her. She fought him off, wailing on his chest.

Abruptly I stopped the car and turned around in the seat. I had had enough.

"Listen here, bitch." Tommy looked like he was talking in slow motion. "Drive you stupid cabby bitch."

"Tommy!" the girl yelled. He backhanded her.

"Tommy is it?" I waved my little confidence in the air between the front and back seat. "Me and my little buddy think it's time for you to get out of my taxi."

Tommy's eyes grew big and I wasn't sure, but I'd put money on it that he just might have shit a little in his shorts.

The next thing I knew, the back door slammed and I was driving full speed.

"That was awesome!" The girl smiled from ear-to-ear. "You just saved my life!"

"What?" I blinked and tried to steady my shaking hands. "No. I didn't save your life." There was nothing worse than seeing a young girl who wasn't able to take care of herself. I guess I was lucky since I had no choice. "You need to value yourself so much more than that. Haven't I seen you at Friendship Baptist on Sundays?"

"Yes," the young girl said meekly.

"Get rid of Tommy and get back to your family and friends and church." Even if it was with Pastor Wilson, anything was better than what she was doing now.

"Thank you," she whispered and turned around and looked out the back window.

Tommy was flailing his middle fingers in the air and shouting something. I slammed on the brakes. He did a double take and took off running when he saw the reverse lights go on because I was going to go back and bust his balls.

"You know," she yammered on, "he treats me like a piece of meat. I knew he only wanted me to go on the docks to get a piece of my ass. I wasn't about it." She smacked the back of the seat, causing me to jump.

I took in a deep breath. She grinned ear-to-ear.

"Are you like some undercover cop or something? Because you are one badass." She nodded her head up and down.

I held up the gun. "Something like that."

After she got out of the car, I gripped the steering wheel and pulled out of the girl's trailer park and headed south on River Road. I was going to cut over on Fifth Street and then left on Main so I could head out of town toward the old orphanage. The state never tore it down and I knew the records weren't ever moved because Trixie would have complained about it in some sort of fashion.

The gravel spit up under the Belvedere tires as I sped up the old drive. There was no reason to try to be careful and not ding the car because after all this FBI stuff, I was going to get a real job and get the Old Girl painted something other than yellow.

I parked the car directly in front of the office window on the left side of the orphanage and left the lights on. Without a flashlight, I had to get creative somehow. Trixie would sit in the bay window and look out as all of us spent our day playing in the front yard. There were always stacks upon stacks of files and manila envelopes. Surely there was something in there with my name on it.

The old stone mansion used to be gorgeous with the ivy growing up the big pillars and the pointy roof. There were eleven bedrooms. Five on each side of the stairs with a master smack dab in the middle. I swear Trixie never slept. She could hear a mouse scurrying around for a crumb at night. If you wanted to sneak out, it had to be after dinner or right after school.

Pieces of the stone steps crumbled with each step I took. The shutters creaked in the night wind. The hair on my arms stood up as the air whipped up and around my body.

"Here goes nothing," I whispered. I'd never been one to be scared of anything, but trying to figure out where I had come from and if I had some sort of diseases was a little terrifying. I couldn't help but have a little fear in my soul. Maybe it was anticipation of finding something about my past that should stay exactly where it was…in the past.

Gia never understood it. As much as I had tried to explain to her, she never had to worry about anything medical or what ethnicity she was. I looked down at my hands wondering if they looked like my mom's and knew I was doing the right thing by trying to figure out something about my past.

The single-pane front door had some broken glass, just enough for me to put my hand in and unlock the door. The old place was dusty and filled with cobwebs.

"Blah, blah." I spit out the cobwebs that had clung on my face as I walked through the large foyer and down the hall to where the office was.

The light of the moon dripped through the large windows, shining into the dark old house putting a little glow in the house.

I peeked my head in all the rooms on the way to the office.

All of the furniture was the still in place as if we had left for a long vacation. With a little bit of dusting, the place would be exactly like I remembered it. The old red velvet Victorian couch and chairs had large tarps draped over them.

There was a sense of belonging putting a little doubt to why I needed to find out about my past. "What the hell is wrong with you?" I closed my eyes and took a deep breath. "Why do you need to know your past? Trixie has been such a good caregiver."

Trixie would be so hurt if she knew I was here, but I had to put that in the back of my mind.

Without thinking too much, I went into the office. The car headlights did exactly what I had intended for them to do. The light was shining in perfectly as though I had the lights inside on. Just out of curiosity I flipped on the light switch. The chandelier flickered right on.

"What the hell?" I continued to flip it off and on as the lights did just that. "Why is the electricity still on?"

That was strange. I knew that Trixie couldn't afford to keep the lights on and the state shut the orphanage down and there was no way they were going to pay to keep the lights on. Something wasn't adding up.

The files were still stacked like I remembered them. The grey filing cabinets lined the inside wall of the room and Trixie's large mahogany desk was still right in front of the window just like I remembered. There was a pen and paper with her handwriting on top as if she had just gotten up to go to the bathroom and would be back to finish whatever it was she was doing.

More and more questions flooded my mind. Why would the electricity be on? Why would the furniture still be here? And why are the files still here?

Regardless, I was there to find out about me, not everything else going on.

One by one the old file doors squeaked when I pulled the long drawers out as far as they would go. There were names on the tabs. Some I recognized and some I didn't. I'm sure they were of kids that had been there long before I was there.

I wasn't sure how long Trixie had run the orphanage before I was born. It was a question I had never asked.

Carefully I used my finger to pluck through all the filing cabinets with no luck to me. I bit my lip and looked around the room. There had to be something somewhere. My eyes zeroed in on Trixie's desk. Vaguely I recalled her always shoving papers in the drawers when I would come in to talk to her.

There were three drawers on each side of the desk and one long one in the middle. Nothing out of the ordinary for a desk. Just a typical wood desk.

I eased myself into Trixie's chair and pulled the top drawer open. Nothing but pens and a few stray paperclips. Then I proceeded to go through each drawer one by one.

"Bingo." My eyes almost popped out of my head when I saw my name printed on a small envelope. "Please be something."

I opened the envelope and pulled out a piece of paper that looked like someone had ripped it off a larger piece of paper.

"Louisville?" The only thing printed on the paper was an address. I was hoping to find something a little more exciting…like Paris, France or something.

I pulled the envelope apart hoping there was something else in there, but there wasn't. I stuffed the piece of paper in my pocket and rummaged through the drawer some more. There wasn't anything else in there but a few unused notepads and unopened pack of pencils.

At least I had an address that I could trace.

## Chapter Thirteen

When I got home, there was a note from Jax Jackson that was slipped under my door. First he wanted to know why I didn't have a cell phone and two he wanted to verify our plan to meet up at The Cracked Egg after I made my drop off with Trigger Finger. He had my first set of instructions.

First set? He had another thing coming to him if he thought I was doing more than one.

Henrietta didn't move an inch throughout the night after we had gotten home from the orphanage, but I did. Trigger Finger Tony, Jax Jackson, having a hand gun, and a possible address from my past rolled around in my head like a hamster on a wheel. And lying in bed didn't help matters.

Thoughts of Trigger Finger pinged in my head only to bounce off an idea about Jax Jackson which made me think about the gun and so on. Nothing was getting solved. Only more of a stomachache which made me wonder if I had some crazy family sickness.

All this talk about Trigger and mobs was taking up all the breathing room for my brain. The whole mobster thing was getting to me.

I surfed the Internet looking at all sorts of images of Trigger Finger Tony. I even saw the guy from the boat and the docks that the caption referred to at Nicoli Fabrizo. He was in a lot of Trigger's pictures, wearing the same head-to-toe white outfit and his finger.

Quickly I got showered, fed Henrietta, and grabbed my bag along with my new little gun friend before I left to go see Derek to get one of his old cell phones he had promised me.

"You're here early." Derek was already in the garage bay working on the same car he had been working on earlier in the week. "Your passenger needs a ride?"

"What? How did you know?" I couldn't believe it. "That Gia!" I was going to give her a piece of my mind for telling him about Trigger Finger.

"Calm down." He wiped his hands off on his already dirty rag. "Why are you getting so worked up? You are the one who told me about Jax Jackson needing a ride to and from Morty's while he's in town for that music festival."

"Oh, yeah." I sucked in a big deep breath, so happy he didn't know about Trigger. I was more on edge than I realized.

The phone rang which caught Derek's attention, taking the focus off of me. He walked in the office to answer it. I heard a few mumbles before he slammed down the phone.

"Got to go!" He ran out of the office with one of his coat sleeves hanging off his shoulder while he tried to finagle the other one on and also shut the bay door. "A little help?"

"What's the rush?" I pushed the remaining opened part of the large garage door down with my foot so he could lock it up on the rail.

"Fresh body!" His eyes sparkled like his toothy grin. "First dead body I'm going to get to see in the line of duty!"

He grabbed his set of truck keys off the hook he had nailed by the door and rushed me out in front of him.

"The phone! I need a phone!" I punched my finger in the air toward the office and watched him run to his truck.

"It's going to have to wait." He jumped into his truck, leaving me standing there.

"Damn." I sauntered back to the Old Girl.

Click, click, click. The sound of a dead battery made me turn around. Click, click, click. Looking through the back of the truck window, I could see Derek smacking the hell out of the steering wheel.

"Piece of shit! Piece of shit!" he screamed and spit on the ground. Not to mention a little stomping.

His eyes slid over to me.

"Laurel, I need a ride." He ran over to the Old Girl and got in the passenger seat without me agreeing to cart him around.

"I'm, I'm…," I looked at my watch. I had to be on time to pick up Trigger or my finger wasn't going to be able to hold that gun Derek let me borrow. I opened the door and got in.

"Drop me off." He put his hands in the air. "That's all I'm asking. River Road!" He pointed ahead.

There weren't any words exchanged between us.

On the way there, he did all the talking about how it was his first case and he couldn't wait to get started on it. Plus he was going to put more hours in at the station and work more nights at the garage. Yada-yada.

"I'll wait right here to make sure I can leave you." I told him before he hopped out of the car—like a kid who just woke up on Christmas—when he saw the group of police gathered on the side of River Road.

He gave me the backward wave. I watched as he walked up to the group. The sheriff seemed to be filling him in on the deets.

I craned my head, trying to see around them. They were definitely interested in something more than just a dead body. Not that a dead body wasn't bad enough. They were all bent down shaking their heads. A few of them covered their mouths.

Not Derek. He stood up and turned around. A big grin planted on his face made his dimples even more adorable. Too bad he was like my brother because he was going to look damn good in a cop uniform.

"You can go on. I'll catch a ride with Jimbo."

Jimbo Warren had been with the police station for over forty years. He should've retired a long time ago, but Susie, his wife, said she'd go crazy if he was home all the time meddling in her business.

It was no business of mine or my tale to tell, but I heard that maybe Jimbo needed to meddle a little more in Susie's business. As he wouldn't be so happy with her extracurricular activities with a certain jailer in our town, Bobby Flynn.

I leaned over and rolled down the passenger window.

"What's going on?" I asked out of curiosity.

"Dead guy. Didn't recognize him." He scratched his head. "His finger is missing."

"Missing?" I asked. My neck ached from the tension that was traveling up my body. "Like his pointer finger?"

"Yeah, how did you know?" he asked and bent down to the window and leaned in on his elbows.

"That's the only finger name I know besides fuck you." Lady like, I put my middle finger up.

"Funny, Laurel." He rolled his eyes. "He's not from here either."

"Don't recognize him and he's dressed funny."

"Funny?"

"One color. Head to toe." He gestured.

"As in white?" My head did flips with the images of Nicoli Fabrizo flipping through my head like a rolodex.

"How did you know?" Derek's eyes narrowed. His brows cast a shadow down his cheeks.

"I could see the sun beating off of something white." I pointed out to the dead body, which I couldn't see, and the sun was nowhere beating down.

"Huh." Derek stared at me a moment too long before he said, "The more I think about it, the more I want you to really stay away from Jax Jackson. He can rent a car. Besides, Trixie wouldn't approve."

"What?" Why would he say such an absurd thing? "You aren't my dad."

"Think about it Laurel." Derek gave me that look. "He shows up to town. Someone turns up dead."

"Oh and he did it." I laughed, though he did plant a seed of doubt in my head. And I couldn't tell him that Jax was an FBI agent. "So when I went to New York City, all the city's homicides should have been pinned on me?"

"Good question if we lived among eight million people." His voice escalated, "Walnut Grove has twelve hundred people."

"I gotta go." I looked at my watch. I had exactly a half hour to get to Trigger Finger or Derek was going to be finding my dead body minus a finger.

## Chapter Fourteen

Now what Derek had said about Jax and the murder being tied wasn't exactly wrong. Jax did tell me about Trigger Finger and Google confirmed it. Plus Jax was in some of those dead FBI agent's funeral photos. So I was going to have to stay on the side of where I was getting paid. The FBI and the mob.

As he had been the last two days, Trigger was waiting in the lobby and came out as soon as he saw my car approaching. Today he was in the same sort of suit but a little more grey. He wore the same slicked back hair, white button up, and rings, minus the finger.

"Good morning, Laurel." He slammed the car door. "I need to go to the church. I have a little sin I need absolved."

"I don't want to hear about it. Lalala!" I sang into the air, images of Nicoli's finger and what I could only imagine his body looked like taking space up in my head. Nicoli's blood wasn't going to be on my hands. The less I knew, the better.

"You women." He shook his head. "That's why I need to go ask for God to forgive me. I had images of me using my little friend on my side piece."

"Oh God, please, please don't tell me about you killing Ni..."

He interrupted, "Just like that." He flung his hand in the air toward me. "She interrupts me all the time. I have no idea why I need a side piece when I have a perfectly well suited ass at home. She knew she was a side piece and I give her a little task and she goes all fucking crazy on me."

"Side piece?" Surely he was talking about his right hand man, Nicoli.

"Yeah, side piece. You know." Loosely he rolled his hand in the air in a circular motion. "Piece of ass...er." He looked at me like he forgot I was a lady. "It's common to keep a mistress in my job."

"What is your job again?" The question flew out of my mouth. There was no way I was going to be able to take that one back.

"You worry about your job of getting me back and forth. Got it?" His jaw clenched. The stress lines between his eyes deepened. "And hopefully it will only be a few more days. I gotta get back to New York. I need a good meatball sandwich." He shook his full hand at me. "That's one thing this little town needs. A good Italian restaurant."

"Is that so?" I asked under my breath. I spoke up a little louder, "I don't know if Pastor Wilson is going to be able to help you."

I wasn't sure Pastor Wilson could help himself, much less a man who had been fornicating with a mistress and wanted to off her.

"I told her. I had bad feelings about my side piece." He stared out of the window.

"Break up with her." It seemed like a simple solution.

"Do you know the thunder Big Manny would stir?" Cough, cough. "I mean, she has a very important family that wouldn't be too happy with me."

"What about your wife? That seems to be the important factor here." To me it was obvious who he needed to take care of.

"I'm done with this conversation," he insisted with returning impatience. Another wad of cash dropped from his fingers, landing with a thud on the seat. I swear it was the biggest stack yet. "Just take me to the church."

There was complete silence until we pulled up in front of Friendship Baptist. I pulled along the side of the curb and put the car in park.

"What the hell is this?" Trigger looked out the window. His nose was curled and his brows furrowed.

"The church." Duh. For a mobster, he wasn't that smart.

"I need a priest!" he spat, spit droplets shooting out of his mouth.

"We…don't have a Catholic church here." I turned around and looked at him.

"Drive," he muttered through gritted teeth and opened up the suit coat showing me his little friend. He said a few more expletives that weren't recognizable, but his tone told me he wasn't happy.

Suddenly I felt numb. Almost paralyzed. There was nothing good coming from this situation. How was I going to defend myself?

I jumped out of my skin and almost pissed myself when someone tapped on my window. My heart fell with relief when I saw Derek standing there. I looked back at Trigger. He gave me a keep-your-mouth-shut look with a little nod. I rolled down the window.

"Hey." I planted a fake grin on my face. Oh no. My heart pounded when I saw Derek was wearing a sheriff's uniform. "Nice duds."

"How do you like me now?" There was pride on his face. "I have to get them altered. Cool though, right?" He held his arms out to show me the fit. "I wish I would have had this on this morning when the Louisville Channel Five News got wind of that dead guy on River Road. They must've burned up the roads getting down here to get the scoop." He ducked down into the window and looked at Trigger. "You here for the festival too?"

"Festival. Yea." Trigger gave one word answers.

"Cool." Derek gave me the stink eye.

"Yea, cool." I took a deep breath. I wished he wouldn't have said anything about Nicoli. "Did you get your truck fixed?"

"Nah. That old thing." He rolled his eyes. "I'm walking over to see Clyde right now to see if he or Baxter has something I can borrow until I get the truck fixed. Are you ready for your big date that Gia mentioned the other night?"

"Shut up, Derek." I pushed his arm off the door. "You better not show up there either."

Ahem. Trigger cleared his throat.

"I gotta go." I waved and smiled.

"See ya, Laurel." Derek tapped the door. "Don't do anything I wouldn't do," he hollered after I drove off.

"Take me to the docks," Trigger demanded. His words were suddenly raw and very angry. "Remember our little agreement, Laurel. No need to be here tonight, but I expect you to pick me up the morning after tomorrow at nine a.m.."

I didn't say a word. There was no way I was able to forget our little agreement. I looked down at my fingers. And I couldn't forget my agreement with the FBI.

"Shit, shit, shit!" I screamed when Trigger got out of the car. I turned the Old Girl back down River Road and headed straight to see Johnny Delgato.

I raked the wad of cash from the passenger seat and stuck it in my bag. The stress was killing me and it was high time I took back my life.

I was going to forget all about Jax Jackson and Trigger Finger Tony. First stop would be to get a new phone, apply at Quick Copy and get my life in order. After all, I was on the up and up, not the way back down. Trigger was going to have to find his own way back to his hotel. When the day was over, I was going to tell Derek everything I knew. Everything I had seen go on at the docks between Morty and Nicoli, along with the FBI plans to use me were all going to go in my file that I was going to give to Derek.

Who could possibly need a phone this early in the morning? I had to park the Old Girl across the street in the K-Mart lot because all of the off-road parking was taken.

"Well, well. If it isn't Laurel London," Johnny Delgato whispered my name, seductively. He flashed his most deadly weapon that I had no defense against. His white teeth.

There was something in a smile that I loved on a guy. His smile was worth a million dollars. They twinkled just as much as his steel blue eyes against his tan skin.

"You bring a double-edged sword." He held his hands to his heart. "Pleasure to look at but painful to know you aren't mine…yet." His eyes narrowed. His chiseled jaw clenched. His stare hurt.

See why I have tried to avoid Johnny Delgato? He makes me lose all my senses.

I reached down in my bag.

"Whoa!" He stuck his hands up in the air. "You don't have any walnuts in there do you? I was just kidding about the hot thing."

"Delgato, I need a phone." I pulled out the five hundred in cash. "If I did have a walnut, I would've already pelted you with it."

For a girl, I had a mean throw. I mean a throw that would hurt someone. In fact, when I got tired of Johnny Delgato's wandering hands, I armed myself with walnuts. I mean the big green walnuts that are all over Walnut Grove, hence the name.

Anyway, I kept a few in my bag and when Johnny Delgato tried to get fresh with any girls at a high school game or even the bowling alley, I'd chuck one right at his head. Most times he'd duck, but once he didn't and got knocked right out. Granted, he had to go to the hospital for a concussion, but it taught him a lesson.

"Did you rob the bank again?" Johnny stepped back. "I don't want any of your dirty money. You can go right on over to K-Mart and buy a phone from them."

"No asshole, I didn't rob the bank. It's my money. Now." I walked over to the counter and pointed to the latest phone. "I want that one and keep the plan I have with my flip."

"I'm going to have to ask Trixie about that because she still pays your bill." An evil grin crossed his lips. "Why is that? Are you still ten?"

"Shut up, Johnny."

"Seriously, Laurel. It's like she's still trying to keep some type of hold on you." He stood with his mouth open, eye narrowed like he was thinking something.

"Hold?" I laughed. "Johnny, she raised me like I was her own. I was the only orphan that never had a foster family or even had a chance to be adopted."

"Hasn't that ever made you wonder way?" he asked a great question. "Even your pal Derek had a few foster families."

"Just get me the damn phone." I shoved him to the right so he could walk around the counter and get my phone. "Call Trixie if you have to. I don't give a shit."

Cautiously, Johnny walked around the counter and took out the phone I had pointed to.

"You think you can handle that particular phone?" The smart assed Johnny was back. I could feel his stare. I didn't look up. "I could come over and show you all the bells and whistles tonight after work," he leaned over the counter, mere inches from my hair and whispered.

"Watch it." I jerked back. I didn't want to make a scene in front of all the people in his store. "Just get me the damn phone."

He smiled. I glared. There was always a sort of sexual tension between the two of us and I would have put money on it that we would have great sex, but it wasn't something I was willing to do. One night stands were Johnny Delgato's trademark. Gia knew all about that.

"Fine." Johnny proceeded to walk around the counter and disappeared into the back room. There was a little window in the wall where you could see a few of his technicians working on customer phones. I watched him take my new phone out of the box. He said something to one of the guys. They both turned and looked at me.

The technician smiled, making me a little uncomfortable. Johnny said something making the guy laugh harder. I wasn't going to pay it any attention. I was just glad the guy put aside whatever it was he was working on and did whatever he needed to do to get my phone working.

Haphazardly I walked around the Phone Shop and thought about what Johnny had said about never being with a foster family or adopted. Granted I was bad, but that was in my later teen years, not the early years when I was cute and didn't know better. What about all those families who wanted an infant? Why wasn't I adopted then?

The questions burned in me, giving me heartburn…or some other disease I might have inherited. 5937 Briar Street rolled around in my head. I couldn't help but think there had to be some sort of answer there. Some clue to my past.

Within a few minutes slick Johnny was back on the showroom floor with my new phone.

"Here you go." He reached out with the phone in his grasp. Our hands touched. Heat gushed to my cheeks. "I'm serious about dinner, Laurel. A little bird did tell me you were using an online dating service."

"Thanks." I plucked the phone from his fingers, careful not to look into his eyes. "Damn Derek."

I was going to kill him when I got my hands on him. Better yet, I would make sure I'd throw my beer on him when I met Bob for cocktails at Benny's. Derek and Johnny were always grabbing a beer. From Bob's picture, he looked like he could take Derek and Johnny down with one swing.

"I've got your number!" he hollered after me. "I'll call you!"

"I'll be sure to ignore you!" I yelled over my shoulder before I pushed the swinging door open and ran across the street to get back in the car.

"Check." I looked down at the fancy phone before I threw it in my bag. "Next thing on the list," I turned the car on, "go meet Jax Jackson and tell him I'm not doing it. There is no way I'm going to be part of the FBI or the mob."

# Chapter Fifteen

"Where have you been?" Jax asked when he jumped in the passenger seat.

"None of your business." I stewed on Derek telling Johnny about my Lunch Date Dot Com activity. Now the entire town was going to know. Johnny Delgato could never keep a secret.

I flashed Louie the bird when I noticed him looking out of the little window from his perch. For a second I thought about getting out of the car and doing some sort dance on the hood like a prostitute, but he'd run and tell Sally who would immediately tell Trixie. So I just flipped him the double bird.

"I thought Trigger had gotten you." He had taken the liberty to sit up front.

"Did I invite you to sit up front?" I asked.

"Um…," Jax was at a loss for words. He changed the subject. "Where have you been?"

"First I had to take Derek to Nicoli Fabrizo's dead body that was found on the side of River Road." I emphasized dead body so he knew I wasn't happy about the situation. I gripped the wheel. "Not far from where we found his finger."

"Nicoli Fabrizo? Are you sure?" Jax's mouth dropped.

Apparently the FBI wasn't as up to date as Walnut Grove Police.

Marvin Gaye seductively sang Let's Get It On from my bag.

"What the hell is that?"

"Ugh." I grabbed my bag and pulled out the new phone. There was a text message from Johnny.

Johnny: Not kidding about dinner. Text me! Hey…did I hear you were prostituting now?

"Stop looking at your phone." Jax grabbed it out of my hands. "Who's Johnny and when did you get a phone? Prostitute?"

"None of your business, none of your business, and none of your business." I snatched it back and put it under my thigh. I proceeded down Main Street and kept going.

"I thought we were going to grab a bite to eat and talk about Trigger." Jax pointed to The Cracked Egg when I zoomed by.

"We need to talk." I took a right on Oak Street and turned left into the Lucky Strikes parking lot next to the

Food Town. I put the car in park and turned in my seat. "After seeing that dead body today, I can't say I'm in any way shape or form ready to do this. I'm stressed. My stomach hearts, I have heartburn and I'm not sleeping. And I don't want to do this."

"That's a shame Laurel. It really is." Jax Jackson's mouth pinched in the corners. "I guess I'm going to have to have you arrested on aiding and abetting the mob in a federal investigation."

He reached around and pulled out his phone. I watched, sure he was trying to bait me.

"I guess I'll call my boss." He tapped his finger on the phone.

"Wait!" Okay so I took the bait. Plus hurting Trixie wasn't on my list of to-dos if he did call the FBI. "I haven't helped them."

"How did you pay for that new phone?" he asked. Silence fell between us. "Thought so."

"So I borrowed a few dollars from the stack." I quipped trying to come up with a better answer.

"Blood money. You used blood money." He used his finger to hen-peck on his phone. He held it up to show me he had dialed a number. “Before I do this, you are sure you don’t want to help out?”

I bit the edge of my lip.

“I need an answer Laurel,” he demanded.

Fatigue oozed from every single pore in my body. I didn’t have it in me to fight the FBI or the mob. It settled in my soul that I was far too deep into this and I didn’t have a choice.

“What do I have to do?” I asked with my eyes fixed on the hood of the car.

“Since Nicoli is dead, there has to be another one of Trigger’s people here.” Jax looked irritated. His fingers fidgeted with a loose string on the side hem of his khakis. “You are going to have to go undercover.”

“That sounded like fun a couple of days ago.”

“What changed?”

I held my pointer finger up in the air. “Oh, I don’t know.” I swallowed hard, lifted my chin and looked at him. “Finding Nicoli’s cold, dead body minus his finger might have something to do with it.”

“I’m not going to let that happen to you.” He reached over and put his hand on mine. “The FBI won’t let that happen to you.”

"I'm already undercover as a taxi driver. And I think I did good covering up who Trigger was when Derek came up to the car and saw Trigger in the back."

"What?" Jax shook his head in an animated gesture. "Derek saw Trigger in your car?"

"Trigger wanted to go to church and when I tried to drop him off in front of Friendship Baptist in the square, Derek was on the sidewalk. Only Trigger wanted a Catholic church to forgive him for thoughts of killing his side piece."

"Side piece? You mean he wanted to be forgiven for killing Nicoli? Did he say that?" Excitement poured out of Jax. Obviously he thought I had something good.

"No, he said he has a side piece, mistress and had thoughts of killing her but he got mad when I asked him what she did. And when he saw Derek in his uniform, it didn't go over well. Plus Derek mentioned finding Nicoli's body."

"Gee." Jax ran his hands through his hair. "We better step up our game."

"What exactly are you looking for? What is it that the FBI thinks is happening here?" It was a question I hadn't even thought about.

"This is top secret and if you ever tell anyone, I will have to deny ever knowing you or ever trying to help you. Do you understand?" His dark eyebrows slanted in a frown.

Slowly I nodded my head.

The corner of his lips turned down. There was a sadness in his voice, "My partner and I got a tip that he was going to run arms through his family's poultry farm which was a great plan since they have trucks going in and out of there. We had been watching him for years and we finally got a tip." Jax put his elbow up on the window and rested his chin on his fist. He looked out the window like he was replaying the scene in his head like a movie. "Somehow Trigger found out and they killed him."

"Then why isn't he behind bars?" Seemed like a very valid question.

"That's not how it works Laurel. When you are dealing with the mob, they get things done and covered up. You can't trust anyone. Not even all FBI agents." His warning chilled me to the core.

"But we are trained to trust the law and those who enforce it."

"Yeah, well." He rubbed his finger and thumb together. "Money shuts people up. Some of the cops could really use a million dollars."

"A million dollars?" For a brief moment I felt like kicking Jax out of my car and rushing to Trigger's side. I could do a lot of damage with a million dollars.

"A million dollars to kill one of our own?" Jax shook his head back and forth.

"If your partner was killed at the poultry farm, it would be reasonable to say that Trigger or someone associated with Trigger did it." Another great question left my mouth. I was feeling a little smarter in the sleuthing department.

"It wasn't on the property." He bit his lip like he was biting back tears. "We were on our way in an unmarked truck, posing as a vendor there to pick up the left-over carcasses. We turned on a street a few blocks from the farm. I saw him. I saw the sniper sitting on the over pass, but Lance didn't want to listen. I screamed at him to turn around." His voice cracked. "He had a look in his eyes that I knew he meant business. He just kept going. The sniper got him right in the middle of the eyes. Instant death," his voice trailed off.

I reached over and put my hand on his thigh. There was a slight jump from him but he didn't look at me.

"I'm sorry. I really am, but aren't they watching you?"

"Nope. The FBI told everyone I was on leave because I wasn't able to handle Rod's death." He looked down at my hand, then his eyes slid to my face. Our eyes locked. "Only I didn't take a leave of absence. I'm working undercover. Following these scumbags wherever they go. Unfortunately that wherever is right here, Walnut Grove, Kentucky."

I pulled my hand away.

He continued, "It's strange they are here. They are bringing more attention to themselves being in a small town, so I have to think he is here on something that is entirely not related to the guns."

"Like what?" I asked.

"I don't know." He rubbed his chin. He glanced over at me. He looked tired, like he hadn't been sleeping. "There is something in Walnut Grove that he wants. And it's not the idea of running illegal weapons through the music festival. That is just a bonus for him."

"How do you know this?" To me all the illegal stuff sounded good. It seemed logical if Trigger wanted to use the river and the warehouse to store his illegal weapons, only and if only Morty was part of it.

I gulped, wondering if Morty knew it was going down right in front of him, but I didn't say it out loud to Jax. Sure I was pissed off at Morty firing me for bogus reasons, but I didn't dislike the guy. Was Morty in on this whole thing with Trigger? Was Trigger going to Porty Morty's when I dropped him off? Gia never said anything about Carmine seeing Trigger. Only the chopstick girl.

"What can I do for you? I need to know." I needed to know for the sake of Morty and Walnut Grove. Instantly I knew I was going to have to make a stop at Porty Morty's. I would come up with some good reason to be there. Maybe see if he'd changed his mind about my job.

"I need a break in his activity."

"What do you mean?"

"All he has been doing is going from the hotel to the docks and back. You taking him back and forth. The FBI doesn't want to tip them off that I'm here, so they are letting Walnut Grove take the lead on the identification of Nicoli Fabrizo."

“That doesn’t make sense.” I knew I wasn’t a super sleuth, but it seemed the FBI would be swarming the place, checking for evidence, fingerprints.

“Perfect sense.” He looked at me like I was stupid. “If he knew we were here, he’d move the operation. I swear he’s planning on using the music festival to smuggle arms.”

“The Underworld Music Festival?” I pretended like I hadn’t already thought of that. My heart sank. Was I right?

This wasn’t helping me take my reputation on the up and up. It seemed I was making an ever bigger, worse name for myself. I could see it now: Laurel London brought the mob to the small town of Walnut Grove, Kentucky.

“Yeah,” he snorted. “Your little note you left at the main office in New York got in his hands and he was all over this little secluded area of the country where no one would ever suspect an illegal arms cartel.”

I tried to swallow the ball that had just lodged in my throat. “The contest sounded great for an economy boost.”

“One of Trigger’s many companies is involved with the Underworld Music Festival’s advertising. As a matter of fact,” He clicked around on his phone. He showed me a picture of a woman with chopsticks in her hair. It had to be the same woman Carmine was talking about. “This is the woman who runs the advertising agency the Underworld Music Festival is using."

"Chopsticks!" I shouted. "Chopsticks has been at Porty Morty's."

"You've seen her? This woman here?" He jabbed the glass screen on his phone.

"No, but Gia's husband Carmine has." My eyes were wide open. "She said that he said a woman who wore chopsticks in her hair, claiming to work with the Underworld Music Festival, is at Porty Morty's working on bringing the festival to Walnut Grove. She's been there twice in the last couple of days."

"Hmm…," Jax bit his lip. "She does own the publicity company for the Underworld Music Festival which is all tied back to the Cardozza family business. But is she working with Trigger to make sure it's here so they can smuggle the arms? That is the question. We need to find out if there is any shipping coming through trucks or boats."

Images of the two white Styrofoam boxes Nicoli had handed Morty popped into my head. Were those filled with firearms? Illegal firearms?

“Wait.” His urgent voice made me come out of my thoughts. “He told you to pick him up at five which means you can go snoop around the hotel for a bit. See if they know the identification of the woman with the chopsticks in her hair.”

“Go!” He interrupted and jabbed his finger toward the windshield. “We don’t have a lot of time between now and five. You have to find out anything you can. I have a feeling his men are moving in and he isn’t going to need you as much.”

“But I have to tell—” I tried to tell him about the boxes I had seen Nicoli give Morty. Maybe it was a lead. Only he refused to listen. He ordered me to step on it, furiously writing something down in that damn notebook of his.

# Chapter Sixteen

Jax had me drop him back off at the Windmill before I could get him to listen to me about the boxes. There had to be something illegal in there. Why else would Nicoli drive up to the dock in a boat and not a car? Why would they exchange heated words?

Jax did say that he had some things he needed to investigate down on the docks since Trigger had told me not to pick him up. So maybe Jax did know about the boxes. Hell, he was with the FBI and I was sure they weren't going to tell me everything they knew.

At least we had a plan in place and it made me feel a little bit better.

I would nose around the hotel and try to see if I saw Trigger come back and who he was talking to. Jax said that anything would be good. And I could be nosey, no problem.

I pulled into the Airport Hotel parking lot and grabbed my bag off the passenger seat. I pulled out my K-Mart, on sale, big-framed sunglasses that took up half my face as if I was undercover. Somehow it made me feel better.

I flung my bag over my shoulder and walked right through the sliding doors.

The atrium of the lobby was amazing. The domed ceiling was like a painting by  Michelangelo. The large pillars and over bloomed flower pots adorned all crevices of the lobby. Marble flooring faded into the marble walls and the shiny gold plated décor stood out.

"Miss, may I help you?" The concierge stood at her podium smiling from ear-to-ear. She held a clipboard close to her chest. "Your name?"

"Umm…," I stammered, unsure of what to do.

"Are you staying with us?" She asked in her petite voice, head slightly tilted to the right, brow cocked.

"I'm not registered yet."

"I can help you with that." She stepped out from behind her podium with her clipboard still in hand. "If you would like to follow me."

"Well, I have some special circumstances that need to be accomodated." I wasn't sure how I was going to figure out what room Trigger was in, but I wanted to be close to him if possible.

"I'm sure we can accommodate." She placed her clipboard on the stand. "Let's start out by the type of room you would like."

"It's not that type of accommodations. I'm undercover," I leaned in closer, "for the Federal Bureau of Investigations." The words dripped out of my mouth like it was something I said every day.

The woman's eyes popped open in delight, encouraging me to go on.

"And there is a man that I'm tailing that is staying here." I made muscle arms. "He has a distinct tattoo of an eagle."

The woman waved her hands in the air. "Headless eagle," she corrected me. She leaned forward. Her eyes shifted side-to-side before they bore into me. "I know exactly who you are talking about." She did a vertical and horizontal assessment of Trigger with her hands.

"That's him," I confirmed. "Anyway, I need to watch him. Watch his moves while he is here. Which means—"

"You need a room near his?" Her eyes narrowed. "This is exciting," she squealed.

"Shhh...," I put my finger up to my mouth. "No one and I mean no one other than you, me, and the FBI can know about this super secret job."

She did the Girl Scout cross-my-heart sign.

"I can put you across from him in the Penthouse Suite B." When she saw me taking out my money, she tapped my hand and shook her head. "I don't know what that slimeball did, but I do know I don't want my hotel's good reputation associated with thugs. You can use the suite free of charge as long as you need it."

"Wonderful." A sigh of relief swept over me. I was glad I was going to be able to come and go as I had pleased, without paying for a room.

"In fact, a woman checked into his room yesterday and she hasn't come out this morning." There was a suspicious tone in her nature. "We had a call on them last night. First they were yelling, then they were you-know-what," she winked, "then they were yelling again. He tried to pay off my security guard to kick the people out next to them. Unfortunately, the other guests left before we could resolve the situation."

"Woman?" I reached for a piece of paper and her pen, "May I?" I asked before she gave me the go ahead to take it. "What did she look like?"

The concierge described a woman with long black hair, tiny waist, enlarged boobs, sky high heels, and tight leather pants while I took notes. "Lots and I mean lots of makeup. You won't miss her. She doesn't look like anyone around here."

"Great." I tapped the piece of paper. I wasn't sure of what I needed to ask next, but I couldn't wait to get to the room so I could get my game plan together. "Did she have chopsticks in her hair?"

"Yes. Strange right?" Her eyes grew big. "They talk funny too. Some sort of northern accent."

"New York?" I asked.

"Never been. Don't know." She squinted. "But I'll be sure to let you know when I see someone coming and going." She put her hand out. "I'm Tammy. At your service."

"Thanks Tammy. Do you happen to know the woman with the chopsticks' name?" I asked.

"I believe he called her Jenn." She squinted like she was digging deep into her memory. "Yes. Jennifer. Jenn." She confirmed.

I pulled the glasses down on the tip of my nose so she could see my eyes. I gave her a long theatrical wink. "What about that room?"

"Yes. That." Nervously Tammy grabbed the two-way off her belt loop and whispered into the walkie-talkie. Within seconds a bellhop was eager and waiting.

"The FBI thanks you for being a wonderful citizen," I said to her before I followed the bellhop to the elevator.

I made sure to throw the FBI in there for good measure. It seemed like the right thing to do and thank God she didn't ask for an ID.

"Just a second." I put my hand on the bellhop. He turned around. "Do you have a business center?"

"Yes, ma'am." He nodded and pointed down another corridor. "Just down through there."

"Great." I rubbed my chin. "I'm with the FBI and I need to make a quick phone call." I pulled out another theatrical wink as to tell him it's all hush-hush. "Do you think we can go down there first?"

"Sure." He changed directions and headed down the hall he had just pointed to.

The gold sign next to the door had Business Center engraved on it. I opened the door and peeked in.

"Good. No one is in there." I turned toward the bellhop. "Do you mind, of course for the FBI, to stand at the door and don't let anyone in here?"

"Yes ma'am." He took his post like a good little soldier.

This FBI stuff was great to use.

I got on the FBI website and looked to see what their badges looked like. Jax flashed his so fast that I didn't get a good look. And if I was going to play the part, I needed a fake badge. Only for the just-in-case-someone-asked-to-see-it situations.

I clicked on an image that I could easily print off and stick it in the Porty Morty lanyard pouch I used for work and just give a quick flash. Like Jax did to me.

I hurried when I heard the bellhop explaining that it would be a couple minutes to someone who wanted in the business center. I knew enough not to leave any evidence behind after I pushed the print button and cropped the picture to the perfect size of my lanyard pouch. With a few simple key strokes, I had erased the memory in the computer hard drive so if anyone came looking, there wasn't a trace I was there. For good measure, I used the edge of my tee to wipe off any fingerprints on the keyboard.

Deep in my bag was my Porty Morty ID lanyard. I stuck the FBI badge in the clear pouch over top of my ID to make it nice and stiff so it did look official. I put it back in my bag, even though I kind of wanted to wear it, but didn't need the attention at this time.

"You ready?" I asked the bellhop.

He smiled and walked ahead of me. There were only two doors on the penthouse level. One was mine and the other had to be Trigger's.

"Here you go." The bellhop opened the door and waited. "Will this be all?"

"Yes." I smiled and waited for him to go, but he stood there. Straight as a stick. "Can I help you with something?"

"Just making sure you liked my service."

He didn't have to say another word. I knew exactly what he meant. I was going to have to pay him for his silence.

"If you need any information about anyone staying at the Airport Hotel, feel free to ask." He smiled and folded up the hundred dollar bill I had given him.

"I see," I said and lifted my head. My eyes met his eyes. We seemed to have an understanding about what was going on. "If I need anything, I'll be sure to ask for…," I glanced at his name tag. "Daniel."

"Yes, ma'am." He turned and headed to the elevator just as the door to Trigger's penthouse flung open.

I ducked a little behind the door in fear they would see me, only the woman didn't pay a bit of attention to me at all. She proceeded down the hall. Her black hair was pulled up in a tight bun with chopsticks stuck in the middle and a black skirt suit topped off with red high heels. She was too busy putting something in her clutch to even bother with me and Daniel.

"Going down?" Daniel asked when she approached him.

"Yes please." She didn't look up from her clutch.

Daniel glanced over her shoulder and gave me a long theatrical wink.

## Chapter Seventeen

Many times I had dreamed of doing nothing all day but sitting in a fancy hotel and being catered to. But the waiting was something I wasn't good at.

I had propped the door open with my shoe and pushed the couch in clear view of Trigger's door so I didn't miss anyone coming and going. The only person I saw was the hotel maid, who also gave me the theatrical wink. Everyone was onto the fact that I was there with the FBI to keep tabs on the other penthouse. Everyone but Trigger, hopefully.

The day was dragging on. I had positioned myself on the couch every which way, even upside down, but nothing was going on. I wasn't sure what Jax wanted to me to do.

I pulled the lanyard out of my bag to get a look at my printed off badge and a piece of paper was tangled up in the string. I opened it.

"Louisville!" I jumped to my feet.

It was the address that I had found in the orphanage office in the envelope with my name on it. I checked my watch. It was lunch time. If Trigger kept to his time of getting picked up at five o'clock, there wouldn't be any action for a while and since I was in Louisville, I might as well go check out the address.

I shut the door behind me and headed down to the lobby where the concierge was ecstatic to see me.

"Today the woman was picked up in an old beat up truck." She smiled and showed me a picture on her camera phone that she had taken. "Did I do good or what?"

"Who was driving?" I asked when I noticed the truck was similar to Derek's.

"A guy I didn't recognize." She bit her lip. "Shoot. I guess I should've gotten his picture too."

"No, you did great." I shrugged off the fact that it wasn't Derek. It couldn't have been. His truck was dead and he wouldn't know Jennifer anyway. I scribbled my phone number on the top of a piece of paper on her clipboard. "Can you text me that picture though?"

I didn't know why I asked her to do that, but it seemed like the official FBI thing to do.

"Yes," she squealed. "Is this evidence?"

"It just might be." I patted her on the arm. "Good work. Let me know if something comes up. I have to run an errand."

We said out goodbyes before I jumped into the Old Girl.

"5937 Briar Street." I used the cool GPS feature on my new phone to maneuver the streets of Louisville.

The further I drove, the shadier the neighborhoods got making me a little happy that I wasn't raised on these streets. With my skills, there would have been no way I would have made it out of here without going to jail.

"59, 59, 59," I repeated as I drove slowly past all the worn-down houses and tried to find the house numbers on them. "593...," I squinted to make out the hand-painted numbers on the chipping overhang on the one that should be the right house.

"5934." I pulled the Belvedere up to the curb wondering if I should go up to the door or not.

It wasn't like it was a guarantee someone who knew me or my past still lived there. Twenty-two years was a lifetime ago for some people. I wrangled with the thoughts in my head, trying to sort through it all.

What if my mom had been a teenager? She'd only be in her late thirties.

A slamming car door caught my attention. A teenage boy with his pants hanging past his butt cheeks was walking away from a late model Chevy Camaro.

“V-6. Manual five speed?” I hollered out to the kid, grabbed my bag, and slammed the Old Girl’s driver’s door behind me. I had to get his attention somehow.

He looked around. His sandy-blond hair flipped behind his shoulder, exposing large gauge earrings in his ear lobes.

“Let me guess.” I walked around the car. “1992?”

“I wish.” He rubbed his hand down the side of the off-white Z-28. “Close. 1991. Though there wasn’t much of a difference.” He walked closer to me. His eyes slid from me to my car then back to me. “In 1992, GM made a major effort to tighten the f-body, with more welds, seam filler, caulking and so forth. The '92s are the quietest and tightest of the 3rd gen line. Not to mention they painted the grill to match the car on the ‘92s.”

Okay. That was way more than I needed to know about his car. I was just trying to make idle chit-chat to get some deets on the house.

“You have a cool car.” He jerked his head back doing the cool thing.

"Thanks." I smiled. Thank goodness I knew a little about cars. It was all because of Derek. He constantly worked on cars at the orphanage. "Hey, do you know who lives here?" I pointed to the house at 5934.

"Nah," he said. "I'm seventeen and nobody has lived there since I was born."

"Hmm." I looked back at the house. It was run down, but it didn't look abandoned run down, if there was such a difference.

"Someone pays the bills because the electricity works."

"How do you know that?" I asked.

"Sometimes me and my friends go over there and you know," he nudged me, "get away from the parental units."

"Oh." I didn't want to know anything more about the "you know" so I decided to use it to my advantage. "I'm here with the FBI. I'm going to pretend I didn't hear you say that and you are going to pretend you didn't see me."

"Bullshit. No fucking way are you with the FBI." He laughed, mouth opened wide showing me his cavity-eaten toothy grin.

"Sure am, buddy." I pulled the lanyard out of my bag and flashed it toward him rather quickly.

"Holy shit, man." He ran his hands through his stringy hair. "Yeah, no. I didn't see you like at all."

"Good." I pushed my way past him and headed up to the front porch of the house.

By the time I got to the top step, the kid had jumped back into his car and zoomed off.

I rubbed a circle spot in one of the dirty windowpanes on the old wooden door and looked in while I jiggled the handle.

I ran off the porch and darted around to the back of the house to look for another way in. A dog from the house on the right ferociously barked from behind a very tall planked privacy fence. The dog had to be some sort of big crazy dog because he sounded like he was going to rip me to shreds if he could get through the fence.

I tiptoed over to the cellar steps and looked down.

"Only a crazy person would walk down there," I said to myself when I looked into the dark space. "And I'm just that crazy." I dug deep for my vote of confidence.

The difference between me now and when I was a teenager, then I didn't even think about the consequences and how it would affect everyone around me.

I took a deep breath and crept down the cellar steps. Once down there I turned the handle of the small wooden door and it was unlocked.

"Hello?" I hollered out.

Before taking another step I felt around in my bag for my gun and held it in front of me. Granted it wasn't steady by any means and if I had to fire, I would probably shoot my own foot, but still. I felt better having it.

Thud!

"I have a gun so you better come out." The feel of the gun in my hands not only made me feel safe, I felt like I was getting some power. Confidence. "Did you hear me you coward?"

Thud!

Shit! I ducked when I heard something big and heavy above my head. The door at the top of the basement stairs leading into the house teetered open, little crumbly plaster fell off the old walls and down the steps, landing at my feet.

How many times had I seen those scary movies where the woman walks up or down the creepy basement stairs only to be slashed into pieces once she got to the end? Here I was walking up the stairs. Was I about to meet my death?

Who knew? But I had a gun.

I used both hands to steady the other with the gun pointed straight ahead and took each step one-by-one. They led right into a little kitchen that was completely outdated, but very clean. There was white tile on the floor. There were a few white cabinets on the wall and the gas stove was small. All the appliances looked to be as old as the house, but in mint condition.

Before I turned the corner of the kitchen, I said a little prayer and jerked around the corner with the gun still pointing, finger on the trigger.

I crept down the small hallway and bolted around the next corner into a family room. The only thing in there was a huge fireplace and mantel.

My whole body tightened, I took a deep breath and dropped my hands to my side when I saw a cat sitting on the mantel. There wasn't any furniture in the house. Definitely abandoned. In good shape, but abandoned.

"Hey, kitty." Stiffly I walked to the fireplace and put my hand out to pat the cat.

The yellow and brown tiger cat jumped down and darted into the depths of the house.

"So maybe none of my family lives here." I surveyed the mantel. "Maybe once there were some pictures on this mantel of my family. I could always go to the courthouse and check the deed records. That would tell me if any Londons ever lived here." I laughed. "If London is my real last name."

At the end of the mantel there was a little key in the wood. Something like a gas log fireplace would have, only there weren't any gas logs in the hearth. I turned the key to see what would happen. A little hidden compartment in the wood opened, exposing a little hidden space.

I stuck my hand in and pulled out a small shell box.

I looked around before I put my gun back in my bag and opened the box.

"What the hell?" I took out a ring that looked to be exactly like one of Trigger's and his posse.

"Laurel?" A voice boomed from behind me.

"AAAA!" I screamed, jumping around with my hands in the air like I was going to do some sort of jujitsu on the guy. I didn't even know jujitsu. I dropped the box, shattering it. Shells went flying all over the place. I plunged my hand deep in my bag. "Don't you come any closer to me. I have a gun! And I'm not afraid to use it!"

"And I was worried about you." He had a slight twisting of the lips. "I knew you were going to be a London through and through."

"What are you talking about?" The gun shook as my whole body rattled in my skin.

"Its okay, Laurel." The stocky man had to be a mobster. Hat, suit, cigar and all.

"It's not okay! Are you one of Trigger's men?" I put two hands on the gun and jabbed it forward. It seemed like the thing to do to give more of an effect. "I don't know who you are and how you know my name, but you better start talking or I'm calling the FBI. I work for the FBI ya' know!"

"I'm not scared of the FBI nor am I scared of you." He drew his hand up to his lips and took a puff of his cigar. With sheer pleasure on his face, he released the smoke into the air. He reached into his coat jacket. "I don't work for the Cardozza family. Anymore."

"I swear I will shoot!" My eyes grew big in anticipation; he was going to draw a gun.

Anymore? What did that mean?

"I'm getting out a business card." He extended his arms to show me. I took it.

"Ben Bassman, attorney-at-law?" I read the card, but still had the gun pointed at him. "What do you want Mr. Bassman?"

"Can you put the gun away and talk to me?" he asked. "Please?"

I stood my ground.

"I knew you were going to come here. Listen." He put his hands out. The cigar dipped up and down from the corner of his lip as he talked. "After years of watching the video stream coming from the orphanage, I was glad to see you finally took the initiative to find out who your people are." He shrugged. "Granted, The Gorilla didn't want you to know and paid me handsomely for keeping it from you. But he always agreed that if you found the secrets, then you should have the family fortune."

It felt like someone had just taken their boot and slammed it into my gut and cut off my breathing.

"I know this is a shock. But I'm here to help. That's what I'm paid to do." He pointed up to the ceiling. "Even if they are paying me from the great beyond. The Gorilla was a man that could see into the future. He wanted what was best for you."

I gulped. My chest heaved up and down.

"This is not real. I fell down. The dog next door attacked me and I'm dead. This is not real." I repeated with my eyes closed tight. Super tight. "I'm going to open my eyes," I warned.

"Still here. Still working for your dead grandfather." The man stuck his hands out to his side like he was showcasing himself. "Your dead mob grandfather, The Gorilla."

"That is not true!" My eyes filled with water. "I have been in an orphanage all my life. My family couldn't raise me. They were poor!"

"And I suppose Trixie told you that?" he asked.

"No, but that is why I was there. I know it!" Many times I would make up reasons my family gave me up for adoption. It had to be money. Had to be.

"Not true Laurel." He shook his head. He put his cigar in his mouth and let it rest in his lips. He walked forward. His long black coat swished. His hands were covered in black leather gloves. "That ring will prove to you where you came from." He pointed to the shattered box and all the contents lying on the floor.

With my eyes still on him, I picked up the ring.

"Go on. Get a good look," he encouraged me. "Plain and simple, I'm here to help you. Protect you because Trixie isn't doing such a good job." He shuffled his feet. "And I pay her handsomely for it too. Well, The Gorilla pays her handsomely."

Letting his words roll around in my head, I looked at the ring.

"This looks like the same ring as the one Trigger Finger Tony Cardozza has." My mind felt cloudy. A headache was in my future. "Wait!" His words started to register in my brain. "You pay Trixie to what?"

"First things first." He pointed outside. "We need to get out of here before someone calls the cops, though Trixie does pay the utilities to keep up the place in case you need it someday."

"Are you telling me that you aren't going to let me leave by myself?" I pinched my arm to make sure this was real.

"You've got the ring." He pointed to my hand. He held out his arms like he was going to hug me. "Welcome to the family."

# Chapter Eighteen

Ben Bassman suggested we meet at a little neighborhood diner around the corner so no one would notice us. I did only because he did seem to have the key to my past.

"Mob? Me? Ring?" Tears stung my eyes as I asked the one word questions over the little café table.

"Your parents," he did the sign of the cross, "were good people."

"Were?" I asked even though he didn't really need to tell me what that meant.

"Unfortunately they were caught in the middle of your grandfather's dispute with the Cardozza family." He picked up the steaming cup of hot coffee the waitress had brought over.

I didn't want anything to drink unless it had pure alcohol in it and nothing on the menu alluded to it so I stuck with a glass of water.

And the more he talked, the more I felt like throwing up.

"The Cardozzas were trying to take over the family business." His silence told me that the family business probably wasn't on the up and up, which was exactly where I was trying to be. "And The Gorilla set up a meetin' at Sal's Pizza, only the meetin' didn't take place."

"Sal's Pizza?" I asked. I had never heard of it.

"Yeah, New Jersey." He snapped his finger. "That's another thing, you are from New Jersey."

"Really?" I was starting to buy into this whole thing before I had even talked to Trixie—who I was going to kill when I got my hands on her.

"While they capped your father, they were over at your house doin' the same thing to Veronica, your mother." He punched his fist in his hand. "The Gorilla was never the same after that. Neither were you. You were a baby. You needed a mother's arms to cuddle you. So The Gorilla did what he thought was best."

"He thought giving me away was protecting me?" I asked. "Here we are today in the throws of danger."

"Trigger has no idea who you are. He only knows that the ring holds the family fortune." He grinned.

"What family fortune?" I asked, vaguely remembering he said something back at the house.

"Blood money." He took a deep breath. "When The Gorilla and the Cardozza put the families together, they had rings made up to signify the union. Only two rings." He pointed to the ring I had snugged on my thumb. "That one and the one Trigger got from his grandfather."

"But—" I started. He interrupted.

"Let me finish." He sighed deeply. "When The Gorilla and the Cardozza made the union, they made one big cartel. One big pot of money. If in the event things went south and one family killed the other, the rings were made."

"So." I shrugged.

"Let me finish." His patience seemed to be wearing thin. He put his hands on the table. "In the event one family would turn on the other for the fortune they had created both rings had to be presented to me, Ben Bassman, in order to get the money."

"You?" I asked.

"I'm the lawyer for both families. New York City no good lawyer." He tilted his head and lifted his hands like what ya gonna do?

"Does Trigger know I'm The Gorilla's granddaughter?" A lump of holy shit sat in my throat. "Is that why he is having me cart him around? Making a plan to kill me?"

"I don't know. It depends on what you have said to him. He knows that The Gorilla's blood grandchild was put in an orphanage somewhere around the Louisville area." He held his arms out in front of him and tugged on the white shirt underneath the sleeves of his coat to readjust. "He fired me months ago because I told him I didn't know where you were and I wouldn't tell him if you were a boy or a girl. Only he wants to kill off the last remaining heir of The Gorilla so he can have all the family fortune."

Everything was becoming crystal clear. "What about the Underworld Music Festival?"

"The Underwhat?"

"He's not here to smuggle his illegal firearms?" I asked.

Slowly he shook his head. "I don't think so. He does all his illegal business through the family poultry farm. At least that was when I was their family lawyer."

"Why do I have to be involved with this?" Suddenly knowing my family history wasn't too appealing.

"Laurel, for the family, you have to kill Trigger Finger Tony and get that ring." The look in his eyes was as serious as a heart attack. “Bring me his ring and get what is owed to you. What your grandfather wanted you to have.”

“I don’t want any blood money.” My stomach started to hurt. “I can’t kill anyone.”

“Let me tell you something.” His words bit like a chilly air whipping through the Kentucky woods in the middle of winter. “When he finds out who you are, and he will find out who you are, don’t think he won’t think twice about offin’ you.”

I gulped.

“Got it?” he asked with a chill in his voice. “Luckily he hasn’t figured out where Trixie is because he will torture her to find out who and where you are. Each day he is getting closer to the truth.”

“But the FBI thinks he is in town to smuggle arms.” I glanced out the window at the beautiful day wondering if it was going to be the last beautiful day I was ever going to see if Trigger was getting closer to figuring out that I’m the one with the ties to the fortune.

“Don’t worry about the FBI.” He leaned back in his chair and stared at me. His voice low, he warned, “You worry about Laurel London. And get that ring.”

Ben Bassman left me the address where he was staying while he was in town and told me I needed to call him on a daily basis to let him know what was going on with Trigger and if I was any closer to getting the ring or making the hit.

I had no intention of making a hit on anyone, but the ring wasn't out of the picture. In my head I had planned to get the ring from his suite while I was undercover for the FBI. How long was it going to take the FBI to realize Trigger wasn't in Walnut Grove to smuggle arms? He was there to find and kill me. I was going to have to play my cards right. I wanted his ring.

The only place I knew where to look was his room in the Airport Hotel. But what if he still had it on? There was only one way to find out…go back.

Some of what Ben Bassman had told me over his lunch made a lot of sense. The past started to add up. There was always enough money for the orphans and me and I figured it was from the state, never my family. I bet Trixie had us dumpster dive for the fun of it. That would totally be something she'd do.

"Good afternoon," the concierge gave me what I refer to as The Baptist Nod.

I had seen Pastor Wilson give it several times. It was the nod where both parties knew what the other meant. So without saying a word, I knew the concierge was telling me that Jennifer was back.

"I think your table in the cocktail lounge is ready for you." She gestured around the six-foot tall potted tree. "If you would like to follow me, Ms. London."

I smiled. I made sure to keep my head down in case Trigger was there. I walked past the bartender who gave the Baptist Nod to the concierge and then gave me a theatrical wink in return.

Obviously it had gotten around the Airport Hotel that I, Laurel London, had been spying on Jennifer for the FBI.

There was a cocktail waiting for me at a table that was positioned with a perfect view of Jennifer. She was on her phone, fussing to someone and enjoying her cosmopolitan.

"Is there anything else I can get for you?" the concierge asked.

"All good. Thank you. You have done enough." I found it a little funny how the fake badge could get so much attention.

Maybe I should tell guys I'm with the FBI. Maybe then I'd get a date.

"Please let me know." She gave one last long wink before she turned around and back around. "Oh, our little friend is going to a little bar in Walnut Grove tonight called Benny's."

I tucked that little bit of information in my head. I watched Jennifer talk on the phone while I got on the Internet with my new phone. I had to get in touch with Bob and set up our cocktail date for tonight. It would be a perfect cover up.

# Chapter Nineteen

There wasn't much going on with Jennifer other than her talking on the phone and her appointment at the Airport Hotel Spa. She was having the two-hour moss body wrap, mud bath, facial, pedicure and manicure. She was going to be there a while.

It was already six p.m. and there was no sense in waiting around. Jennifer was going to be going to Benny's, I wanted to make sure I got there early to get the best bar table. I wasn't sure if Trigger was going to meet her there. Which didn't make much sense if he was trying to keep a low profile since he was smuggling guns and stuff.

Either way. I was going to be there.

I had enough time to go home and feed Henrietta before I got ready for the "date with Bob." It was a good cover up for staying undercover. I decided not to call Jax because I was going on my date and see what Jennifer and Trigger were going to do at Benny's Bar.

Besides, if Trigger knew who Jax was, Jax wouldn't want to show his face anyway. And my new fancy phone had a camera and if anything went down, I'd use it.

I used my phone to email Bob and let him know that tonight was good and to meet me at Benny's Bar at eight o'clock. He was totally down with it and told me he would be carrying a rose so I would know who he was. Little did he know, I had already used the camera on my phone to snap a screen shot of his profile picture on Lunch Date Dot Com so I would knew who he was.

Eight o'clock was a perfect time to grab a table, get a beer and watch the door. Plus it was dollar draft night. The usual going out time was around the nine-thirty, ten o'clock time for a week night. Generally everyone grabbed a quick beer, caught up on the day's gossip, and got home just in time to go to bed so we could do the same thing the next day.

I didn't frequent Benny's a whole lot during the week for the fact that the money I would have spent there had to be spent on other things. Tonight I could spy on Jennifer, get free beer off of Bob, and maybe have a potential boyfriend.

Meow. Henrietta jumped off the futon, stretched her striped grey legs out in front of her and arched her back into a big stretch.

"Hey girl." I bent down and let her run over to me. "Let's eat."

I picked her up and walked over to the kitchenette to get one of the cans Derek had gotten for me from the Dollar Store.

Henrietta sniffed the mashed up stuff and stuck her nose up in the air.

Meow.

Her disapproval was not only in her meow, but the fact she ran back under the futon without eating it told me she was mad. Maybe I could score something from the bar to bring home. Until then she was going to have to suffer and eat it.

The black flirty skirt that hit just above my knees was clean. I paired it with a white tee under my jean jacket and hot pink heels. I threw on a silver ball necklace and earrings to complete the look along with a swipe of lipstick and I was on my way.

Benny's Bar was on the far side of town near Derek's Garage and right before the curve to the old orphanage. It sat right off the road with a gravel parking lot in front.

Jeff Sheffield, owner of Benny's, had bought the land and turned the old barn into the only honky tonk bar in town. He kept the rustic look by repairing the old barn wood by using reclaimed wood from a similar barn. He tore out all the stalls and had the dusty dirt floor replaced with concrete. The bar ran the length of one of the outside walls and different colored vinyl stools butted up to it. A small stage and dance floor was in the back of the barn, which was where local talent could showcase their music or an occasional karaoke contest was held. On any given three-beer night, I might be the up on the stage giving my best rendition of any Carrie Underwood song.

Tonight. Tonight I was going to be on my best behavior.

"Well, well, well." Johnny Delgato swiveled his stool to face me when I walked into Benny's. A grin tipped the corners of his lips. "Are you here to take me up on my offer?"

"You wish." I didn't bother making eye contact with him.

If I did pay him any attention, all of my senses would probably revert back to the sixteen-year-old girl who secretly wanted to do all the naughty things he was always suggesting, that was until I knocked him out with that walnut.

I scanned the café tables to find the best view of the entire bar. The two top in the far right corner was probably the best shot since it was not directly under a light, a little dim, and I could almost hide myself behind one of the stage speakers, only it sat off the stage on a tri-pod.

"Laurel," Derek rotated the stool that was next to Johnny. "Did you get your job back at Porty Morty's?"

"Why would you think that?" I briefly stopped, but still kept my eye on the table.

"Since you are driving around two people with the festival, I figured you conned your way back into your job." Derek dragged his chilled mug closer to him.

He used his fingernail to make marks in the frost on the glass before he picked it up to take a drink.

"Oh no. Not yet." The less I said, the better it was for all involved. "I'm working on it." I added to make sure he stayed off the mob and FBI trail.

There was no need to for him to go all postal cop on me.

"Have a seat." Derek patted the open stool next to him.

Derek put his finger up and motioned for Jeff, who was behind the bar, to grab me a frosty mug.

“Mug or can?” Jeff yelled over Tim McGraw professing his love through the speakers of the jukebox.

“Mug,” I said and then turned to Derek. Johnny was hunched over his beer with a big smile on his face. He winked. My stomach curled. “I’m going to grab a table tonight.”

“Why?” Derek’s brows dipped.

“Because I don’t want to sit by him when you leave.” I tilted my head Johnny’s way.

I was relying on Derek’s track record of having one beer and leaving so he wouldn’t even be there when Bob got there. The date would be on the down low, which was where I wanted it to be.

“Even though you don’t have to be at Porty Morty’s in the morning, you should still get up and put out applications.” Derek was playing the big brother role. “You still have to have money.”

Jeff put the beer in front of me. Before I could dig out a dollar for the beer, Johnny slapped down a five dollar bill.

“I’ll pay since you haven’t said yes to my text. Yet.” He winked.

I reached over Derek’s hands and mug and pushed the money back toward Johnny.

"I don't need your charity."

He started to protest, but Derek stood up.

"Buddy," he smacked Johnny on the back, "you can forget it. Once Laurel makes up her mind, it's made up."

"And don't you forget it." I slapped my dollar down and grabbed the thick glass handle.

Derek pulled a dollar out of the front pocket of his jeans.

"You will." Johnny chirped to my back as I made my way over to the table. "I will be feeding you grapes in bed."

Inwardly I groaned. He was just trying to get my goat and I wasn't going to fall for it like every other girl in Walnut Grove had.

"Just ignore him. He knows he's getting on your nerve." Derek gave that smile that melted every girl's heart, but I knew it as the big brother smile. "I'm going to go to the bathroom and then heading out."

"Okay. I'm going to have one and head home too." I lied trying to throw off his inert cop sense. "I'll let you know how the applications go."

"Alright." He smiled. "How is the car?"

I glanced over his shoulder when I saw a guy holding a rose walk in. A balding, scrawny guy with a rose.

My eyes grew big and I jerked my head in line with Derek's, praying against all hope that the balding guy with the rose was not Bob and just a happy coincidence someone else was getting a rose besides me.

"Good. The car is great." I patted his arm to rush him along. If that was Lunch Date Date Dot Com Bob, I didn't want Derek seeing him. "Well, going to go drink my beer while it's cold."

"Ohhkay," he said.

Shoo. Relief settled in my stomach as I watched Derek disappear into the boy's bathroom. I ducked behind the speaker and watched as Bob walked around.

"Shit, shit, shit. No," I moaned when Bob stood next to Johnny saying something to Jeff.

Jeff pointed my way. Bob's eyes slid over to me. Behind him, Johnny Delgato leaned back on his stool, looked me straight in the eye, and smiled like he had just made a date with the devil.

# Chapter Twenty

"Are you Laurel?" Bob asked.

"Yes," I whispered hoping I could just melt into the seat. "Are you Bob?"

"Have the rose to prove it." He held it in the air. Nervously he ran his hand over his Mr. Clean bald head. His eyes squinted. "Wow, you look just like your picture."

"That would be one of the requirements of the dating site." I grabbed my beer and took a big gulp.

The site specifically said to put an updated picture on your profile page. Bob must've missed that little bit of important information.

"I guess I can't say that I have lost a little muscle over the past few days." He laughed out loud like it was some sort of joke.

Only I wasn't laughing.

I caught a quick glance of Johnny. He was laughing and telling Derek about Bob. Derek turned around, but I looked away.

“Yeah.” He let out a big sigh when he saw I wasn’t amused. He sat down without me inviting him. “That was a really old photo.”

I cocked a brow.

“In the nineties old. I’m also in my fifties.” Deep set worry formed in the lines around his eyes.

“There she is!” Trixie pointed and yelled from the front of the bar with Jax Jackson next to her. Both of them had a tin foil hat on.

Out of the corner of my eye, I saw Derek take his seat on the stool and Trixie walking Jax over to me.

I looked under the table to see if I could fit under it or if there happened to be a trap door I could use to escape.

“What is the use of having a phone if you aren’t going to answer it, young lady?” Trixie’s eyes darted back and forth between me and Bob. “And drinking with a stranger? Are you sure Louie isn’t telling me the truth about you prostituting? Thankfully Pepper was leaving the bank and we hitched a ride from her.”

Trixie glared at Bob the whole time. Her tin foil hat sat cockeyed on top of her head. Jax assumed the same pose. Both staring Bob up and down.

"Ma-maybe I need to go." Bob jumped out of the chair, knocking it on the ground. He scurried off and I didn't try to stop him.

"I realized I didn't have your number so I went to your apartment and this wonderful young woman was there." Jax's dimples deepened. His blue eyes dug deep in my heart causing me to take several short breaths. His five o'clock shadow had definitely turned into an eight o'clock sexy shadow.

"Nice hat." I dragged my mug toward me and took a drink.

I took a bigger drink when I saw Bob sit in the open bar stool next to Johnny and Derek sit right back down again. Jeff was laughing and filling all of their mugs.

"I hear the aliens might be coming." Jax grinned.

"You are a charmer." Trixie must've had invisible strings connected from her shoulders, lips, and brows because they all lifted in delight in the same time. "So who was that old man?"

"He was a date. A legitimate date that you scared off." I rolled my eyes.

The embarrassment was killing me. I tucked a strand of hair behind my ear and shook my head.

My eyes slid back over to the bar to see what Derek and the boys were doing.

"Oh my God." I gasped when I saw Jennifer, chopstick Jennifer, walk into the bar on Morty Shelton's arm.

Trixie and Jax turned to see what I had almost fainted over.

"Thank you for bringing me to her." Jax nodded at Trixie. "We need to talk about the Underworld Music Festival, right?"

He looked at me. I knew he was trying to get Trixie out of here.

"Yes." I stood up and put my hands on her arms, turning her toward me. "Now," I grabbed the tin foil hat off of Jax's head. It took all I had not to run my hands through his thick black hair. He had the perfect luscious hair with enough gel to make it a little shiny. "Derek is on his way home so grab a ride with him."

"You take care of her." Trixie's eyes softened when she looked at Jax.

"You know I will Ms. Trixie," Jax said, letting that northern accent do unmentionable things to me and Trixie.

"You be sure to come over for some bean soup and cornbread. I have the best onions in my garden." Trixie's smile was longer than the Kentucky River.

"You'd better go." I nodded toward Derek and the boys who were still turned in their stools watching us. I gave her the tin foil hat.

Jax and I stood in silence until Derek got off his stool and escorted Trixie out of Benny's.

"Another date down the tubes?" Jax laughed so loud the entire crowd that had gathered in the bar turned to look at us. Even Jennifer.

"Stop being so loud. She's going to recognize you." I pulled him into the shadow of the speakers.

"Why didn't you tell me she was coming here?" He looked me square in the eyes. Charming Jax was no longer around. "You are working for us now. You have to tell us your every move."

He took in a deep breath. I lifted my hand when I caught Jeff's eye and held up two fingers.

"And it seems that everyone at Airport Hotel knows who you are and what you are doing there." He shook his head. Disappointment settled on his face. His jaw tensed.

"This is official business, Laurel. You have to start taking this seriously or you are going to get me and you killed."

"Listen," I put my hands up in front of me and reclined back in my chair. "You told me to watch her. I did the best I could. I only have my street smarts to rely on, not some fancy FBI degree."

"You," he stopped talking when Jeff put two mugs on the table.

"Two dollars." Jeff waited.

"Aren't you paying? This is a business meeting right?" Jax asked. "I'm here for you."

He had me there. If I was going around telling everyone that Jax was here for The Underworld Music Festival, it was only right the host pay.

My lashes lowered. I scowled at him and dug into my bag to pull out a couple dollars. I slapped them in Jeff's hand.

"You are such a gentleman," I leaned over the table and whispered over the mugs. "Besides, I had a date set up for tonight."

"I had to show the concierge my FBI badge to prove I was with the agency. Nice move on the badge." His eyes stared at me over the mug as he took a drink.

Normally I would think that was very seductive, but not right now. I gulped and looked around. Jennifer and Morty had taken a seat at a table across from us. I knew neither of them could see me. To be sure, I scooted my chair a little bit more behind the speaker.

"The concierge told me all about Jennifer's, that her name right?" he asked. I nodded. "Jennifer's day at the spa and she was coming here tonight. So when I couldn't find you, I thought Trigger had seen you there doing what you called spying and killed you. I realized we hadn't exchanged numbers and went to your apartment where I found the lovely Trixie." He took another drink of his beer. "She's really charming."

"Leave Trixie out of this." I warned him she was off limits.

"She is and I told you I would keep you both safe if you didn't try any crap." He slammed the mug down. "This little stunt is crap, Laurel. Dangerous."

Morty and Jennifer got up and walked out of the bar.

"This is not the time to scold me." I jumped up to follow them out, leaving Jax.

When I got to the door, I could see that Morty was walking Jennifer to his car that was parked on the corner of the barn. I rushed around the barn and hid in the shadow on the corner.

Morty and Jennifer leaned up against my old company car. I nearly jumped out of my skin when I felt hot breath on my neck.

"Can you hear them?" Jax was so close. Too close.

A shiver of awareness sent electric shocks through me. I wanted to chalk it up to the adrenaline from spying on Morty and Jennifer, but I knew it was the fact that Jax's body was less than an inch from mine. His palm was pressed on the side of the barn and he leaned closer to me. If that was possible. His body so close it made me hotter than the cast iron skillet Trixie used to make her cornbread.

"Stop talking," I whispered, trying to get my head back in the game. I had to stop thinking about Jax Jackson in the way I had hoped to think of Lunch Date Dot Com Bob.

"This is my home," Morty raised his hands in the air. "I won't let this happen."

"You don't have a choice. I'm not sure when it's going to happen, but it's going to happen." Jennifer warned. "If you don't cooperate, bad things will happen."

"When is he coming?" There was fear in Morty's voice.

There were a few more mumbles before they hopped in the car and took off.

"It's going down." Jax jumped around. Obviously his adrenaline was from Morty and Jennifer. Mine…not so much. "This is it, Laurel!" He grabbed me, pulling me into his arms. "This is it!"

I took a deep breath trying to gather my wits. Jax's smell of soap, gel, and sexy man made me even more dizzy.

"Aren't you excited?" he asked.

His lips were so close.

"I. . .," I fumbled with words. There had never been a time that I was at a loss for words.

"Are you okay?" He asked, looking deep into my eyes still holding me close. "I mean, if you aren't, I don't want to risk your health."

I jerked away and stepped back. Ahem. I cleared my throat and tugged at the ends of my jean jacket.

"Of course I'm okay." I shrugged off the notion and took a deep breath to clear my cluttered head. "Yes. It's going down."

"This is great." He paced back and forth rubbing his hands together. "Tomorrow he might say something or have you change when and where you pick him up. He probably had Jennifer laying the ground work and he is now going in for the kill."

It made sense. Morty was a sucker for a good looking woman and if he thought Jennifer was there for the festival I was sure he was sweet talking her. Little did he realize that she was using him. But what about Nicoli and those boxes I had seen them exchange that day on the docks?

"Nicoli—" I started to tell him about the boxes but he interrupted me.

"What time are you picking Trigger up?" He checked his watch.

"I'm not. But Nicoli—" He interrupted again.

"What do you mean you aren't?" Jax stepped into the moonlight. His eyes glowed like one of the stars that dotted the beautiful night sky.

"He…he," I shook my head to make myself stop looking at him. "He said that he didn't need me tomorrow, but the next day pick him put at the hotel at our normal nine a.m. time."

"Okay." Jax bit the side of his lip. "What is your number?"

I spouted out my digits as he put them in his phone.

"I'll give you a call and let you know our plan in the morning." He started to walk backward toward the road. "Thanks, Laurel! The agency is indebted to you."

"Do you need a ride?" I asked as I watched him turn to jog on the road.

"Nah! I have to run off the adrenaline." He disappeared into the night.

"I have a better idea to work it off," I muttered with images of Jax in my bed running through my head.

## Chapter Twenty One

Since I wasn't picking up Trigger, I had taken Henrietta for a quick walk and taken my profile off of Lunch Date Dot Com. I wasn't going to go through another disaster. Besides, it seemed like my little job for the FBI was coming to an end and I really needed to find a real job.

To waste time until I heard from Jax, I decided to call Trixie. I knew she was dying to know what all last night at Benny's was about. And I wanted to see if she wanted to have lunch so we could discuss everything Ben Bassman had told me.

"Speak to me," Trixie answered her phone.

"What's going on?" I asked her while I was on my way back to the Airport Hotel to do what Jax asked me to do and to see if I could get in there while Jennifer was gone. Hopefully she was still gone.

"Nothing much. Just watching a little boob tube. I see you got a new phone." She made the observation.

"I did. Johnny said he had to clear it through you." Come to think of it, it would be nice to be wealthy and not rely on Trixie to give permission. “By the way,” I took a deep breath. “I know all about my past.”

Cough, cough. Trixie gasped for air on the other side.

“Don’t fake with me.” I was going to ignore her ways of avoiding the subject. “I know I’m from New Jersey. The Gorilla is my grandfather. And you know that the guy I have been driving around is a guy from the family that The Gorilla had been trying to keep me safe from. Well he’s here and he’s going to kill me. Maybe us. So you need to—”

“Who are you? What do you want?” Trixie screamed into the phone before it went dead.

“Trixie? Trixie?” I screamed into the dead phone knowing exactly what was going on at her house. “Shit! Shit!”

I jerked the Old Girl to the side of the road and dialed Derek’s number.

“Shit,” I groaned when his voicemail picked up.

“Leave me a message.” His voicemail beeped.

“Derek,” I gasped. “You have got to go to Trixie’s house. It’s an emergency. The mob is in town and they have her. Long story! Hurry before it’s too late!”

Throwing the car in gear, I pushed the pedal to the floor.

"Let's see what you got." I gripped the wheel and took the roads as fast as I could back into Walnut Grove and along the curves of River Road.

I had a gun. I had a car. And I was going to save Trixie with or without Derek's help. For a second I could imagine Trixie taking down Trigger and she would have if she'd known he was coming for her.

Trixie wasn't one to mess with. I had seen her pull out her shotgun and stare down the barrel many times at total strangers when they would pull up the old gravel driveway at the orphanage. Which makes sense now that I knew she was always looking over her shoulder because of The Gorilla…my grandfather.

The honking horn behind me caught me off guard. I looked through the rearview mirror and tried to go a little faster when I noticed it was Johnny Delgato. He was the last person I needed to be bothered with right now.

It didn't look like I was going to shake him because he tailed me the entire way to Trixie's. The Old Girl did a fishtail into her driveway and I barely got the car in park before I had jumped out with my gun snug in my hand.

The driveway was clear and Trixie's door was wide open. I could hear her television turned up.

"What the hell are you doing, Laurel London?" Johnny screamed. I heard his car door slam and his loud footsteps getting closer. "You are going to kill someone. Is that a gun?"

I had planted myself next to the door and the gun pointed up, tight to my chest. I was going to go in flailing my gun.

"Laurel, put the gun down. Trixie did the best she could." Johnny tried talking me off the ledge.

"Shh." I put a finger up to my lips, almost giving myself a fat lip when my thumb with the big fat mob-family-crest ring bumped it.

In one big move, I flung the gun in front of me with my arms extended and turned the corner into Trixie's house.

"Trixie?" I screamed and scanned the family room with my gun swooping in front of me.

I noticed there was only one leopard print slipper next to her high-heeled styled lounger where she watched her television shows. Her TV tray, where she generally ate her dinner and kept her remote control, was tipped over with everything scattered. Including her word puzzle books.

"What the hell is going on?" Johnny propped himself up against the door frame and gasped for air. "Put that damn thing down. I won't ask for another date again. I swear."

"Shut up, Johnny." I walked down the hall. The hole was getting deeper in my heart as I realized Trixie wasn't there.

"Laurel," Johnny continued to speak, annoying me even more. "What is going on here?"

"Call Derek!" I screamed from the back of the house as I checked every room to make sure she wasn't lying somewhere dead. "Call the cops! Tell them to get to Morty's now!"

"Okay." Johnny didn't ask any questions which was good because I just might have to use my one and only bullet to get him the hell out of my way.

When I didn't find Trixie anywhere, I even checked out back in her chicken coop, I ran around the front and jumped back into the Belvedere. Only Johnny was in the way.

I beeped the horn several times before Johnny came out.

"I didn't know you were out here." He threw his hands in the air.

He moved his car and got out, standing in my way.

"Get out of my way!" I shouted and motioned for him to move.

He moved alright. He jumped right in.

"What the hell are you doing?"

"I'm not sure what is going on, but I have a feeling something bad is going down and I'm not going to let you go by yourself." Johnny reached around for a seatbelt, but it was an old car so the seatbelt was the lap kind.

"I'm not dragging you into this." I refused to move the car. "Get out now!"

"No." He folded his arms in front of him and stared ahead.

"Johnny, get out now," I said through my gritted teeth. "Or I'm going to use my friend on you," I threatened.

"Then you will have to drag my dead, bloody body with you." He didn't budge.

"Asshole!" I pulled down the gear to drive and peeled out of the driveway.

"What is going on?" Johnny asked, holding on for his life as I slid through all the stop signs on the way into town and down Main Street straight for the Windmill.

Jax had never given me his phone number last night. We had only made times and places to meet. He was my only hope. The FBI was my only hope.

"Johnny, there are bad people in town who want to hurt me." I squinted trying to hold my lane as the car squealed onto Main. "They are from my past. Way past. As in I never knew them but they need me to enhance their life." I tried to keep all the privacy I could because I didn't want Johnny to know my business until I got to the police or FBI.

"What do you mean?" His jaw hardened.

"Just take my word for it. I don't have time to explain right now. Did you get a hold of Derek or the police?" I asked and screeched into the Windmill abruptly stopping at the lobby door.

"I left Derek a message and told the dispatch to go to Porty Morty's."

"Shit! Where is Louie?" My head darted around looking for any signs of the big guy.

The doughnut truck was there and so was his car so I knew he had to be there somewhere.

"I'll be right back." I jumped out of the car and ran into the lobby.

The Windmill wasn't in the twenty-first century. They still used the old ledgers to check in guests. Old keys hung up behind the counter with the room number engraved on them and only one of them was missing. Room five. Jax Jackson's. It had to be. There wasn't anyone else staying there.

I ran out of the lobby and down the covered sidewalk to room five. I beat on the door.

"Jax! Jax, are you in there?" I beat harder, even though I knew the room was empty.

I put my ear to the door. Nothing. Just for kicks, I turned the knob. It was unlocked.

I looked back at the car. Johnny was turned around looking back at me so it made me feel better knowing that if I went in and something happened, Johnny might have enough sense to come help.

I pushed the door all the way open with my toe. The room was a mess. The tall floor light was knocked over, the light bulb smashed into tiny glass pieces all over the shag carpet. The bed covers were ripped off the bed and thrown all over the room. Even the glasses were shattered on the floor as if someone had thrown them at the wall.

Jax had to have been taken like Trixie was…forcibly.

"Ohmygod!" I turned to go back to the car and ran straight into Johnny…actually ran into his muscular chest. "You scared the shit out of me!"

"You disappeared into this room and it took a minute so it freaked me out." Johnny's eyes were wide open with apparent worry on his face. "You have to tell me what is going on."

"We have to go to Porty Morty's." There wasn't anything else I could think of. I walked back to the car. "But my one bullet isn't going to stand a chance against Trigger Finger's gun."

"Trigger Finger? Gun?" Johnny grabbed me by the arm and stopped me dead in my tracks. "Enough." He dangled my keys from his finger. "You aren't going anywhere until you tell me exactly what is going on around here."

"Fine!" My hand soared through the air when he jerked his back as I tried to swipe the keys back. "Give me the keys and I can explain on the way."

Reluctantly he handed the keys over. I snatched them before he changed his mind.

"You don't happen to have a gun do you?" I asked hoping he might be packing.

"No, Laurel. I'm a phone guy." He wasn't amused. "Now, what is going on?"

"I got fired from Porty Morty's a couple of days ago. Derek gave me this car. A mob guy thought I was a taxi and jumped in. He hired me to be his driver like they have in New York City and I accepted. Big bucks." I rubbed my finger and thumb together. I stuck with just the main details because I had limited time to catch him up. "Jax Jackson is an FBI agent and has been watching the mob guy whose name is Trigger Finger. Has piranhas that eat fingers…," I batted my hand in the air. "Long story. Anyway," I continued, "Trigger is after me because of my biological family and the FBI doesn't know that. They think he is here because he might be smuggling guns. I'm working for the mob and the FBI."

"Wait…" He laughed.

"You think this is funny?" I glared at him while trying to keep my eyes on the road.

"No, but you are working for the FBI when you are a criminal?"

"I think you can use that term loosely. But why not?" I asked. "I'm good at doing a little con stuff here and there, plus Trigger Finger trusts me. If he only knew I was the one he was after," I murmured.

"This Trigger Finger guy doesn't even know you are the one he's here for?"

Slowly I nodded my head. Off in the distance I could see the big port-a-let sign that read Porty Morty's. My heart pounded as we got closer.

"He figured out that Trixie was the headmaster which leads me to believe he kidnapped her because he knew I would find out."

"But he doesn't know it's you?" Johnny looked all sorts of confused.

"Something like that. Now that I've seen Jax Jackson's room all torn up and Louie no where to be found, I'm thinking Trigger has them too. And maybe they are all at Morty's." I slowed down to pull in.

There were no police cars there and I didn't see Derek's truck. He should've fixed it by now.

"Don't pull in," Johnny ordered. "You said Jax Jackson is with the FBI?"

"Yes," I confirmed and hesitated before I continued driving the car north on River Road passing Porty Morty's.

"My college roommate is head of the FBI in Louisville. I think we should go there and see him about this because all of this is way over our heads." He reached over and touched my leg. "Laurel, I don't think I could bear it if we went in there, especially with your one bullet, and something happened to you."

"What about Trixie?" My voice quivered.

I had never heard Johnny Delgato ever speak with a lick of sense and what he was suggesting was a great idea.

"Trixie will be fine. She's pretty kick ass herself." He wasn't lying. I could imagine her in there giving them the business. "It won't take us a half an hour. I'll even call Mike to let him know we are on our way."

I took a deep breath and did what Johnny told me. It sounded like a solid plan and something Jax would probably want me to do, so I kept going and headed north to Louisville.

The entire drive my stomach curled. I couldn't help but think Trigger had Jax and Derek. Especially since Trigger knew Derek was with the police department and had mentioned Nicoli's body when Derek had approached us while we were parked in front of Friendship Baptist.

# Chapter Twenty Two

"Mike said that Trigger Finger Anthony Cardozza is the biggest mob boss in the United States." Johnny gripped his phone. "He said that we are doing the right thing by coming to the office and taking your statement. He even said that he called and got some men ready to go."

"Oh Johnny, I don't know how to thank you." I looked over at Johnny and completely saw him in a different way.

Though he'd always been handsome, he was even more attractive now that I had seen he had in fact grown up.

"Don't worry about that now, Laurel." He chewed on his bottom lip. "We need to find Trixie. Let me call Derek again."

The traffic in Louisville wasn't bad and I followed Johnny's finger directions as he continued to try to get in touch with Derek.

"No luck." He shook his head. "What is in your past that makes this guy want you?"

"You aren't going to believe it if I told you." I wasn't sure what I was able to say and Ben Bassman told me not to say a word to anyone. "But evidently my parents were killed in some big mob hit right after my grandfather and Trigger Finger's grandfather brought our two mob families together to form one big cartel. Only Trigger's family got greedy. My grandfather thought I'd be safe in Kentucky, of all places." I left out the Trixie part, along with the rings and money. "Needless to say, I think he's here on some unfinished business that I have nothing to do with."

I felt my front jean pocket for the ring.

"What kind of business?"

I shrugged, "No clue." I lied because I just didn't know what was true with Ben Bassman's story and what wasn't. All I knew was that something had happened to Trixie and Jax which made me think some of Ben's tale was accurate.

"This is crazy." Johnny ran his hand through his hair. "Right here." He pointed to a spot on the street.

"Why don't we park in the parking garage?" I asked what seemed to be a logical question.

"Because Mike said to park here, next to the building." He pointed to the door across the street that had the FBI logo on it.

I pulled in and parked. I got out of the car and bolted across the street.

"He said to go in the side door!" Johnny screamed, but it was too late. I had already run into the front of the building.

"I'm Laurel London and I need help! Trigger Finger Anthony Cardozza has my Trixie and FBI agent Jax Jackson held hostage and I think they are at Porty Morty's warehouse in Walnut Grove." I spouted out to the FBI agent that was sitting at a desk in the lobby.

I bent over with my hands planted on my knees to get my breath. Johnny ran up behind me.

"We are here to see Mike Florenza," he told the guy.

The guy gave me a sideways glance, raised his brows and picked up the telephone. He whispered a few things in the receiver and put the phone down back on the receiver.

"Mike is coming down." He pointed to the chairs in the lobby. "You can wait over there.'

"Where are the agents with the gun? Equipment on?" I begged to know.

"Laurel, that happens in the movies. Just calm down. Mike will handle it from here." He pulled me over to the chairs.

We barely had enough time for our butts to hit the leather seats before Mike came running down the glass staircase that took up most of the lobby.

"Come on," he ordered and we followed. "Tell me everything you know," he said when we got into the big conference room. He put a tape recorder on the table and pushed a few buttons.

"We don't have time for this!" I screamed and beat my palm on the table. "Trixie is in danger!"

"Laurel London, is it?" he asked with his jaw tensed. "We can't go in guns blazing without getting all the right information needed. Understand?"

"Yes," I calmly said and began to tell my story from the beginning. I didn't see the need to tell him about the ring or the money because that didn't seem to matter.

"Laurel, you wait here and I will take this to the guys who are waiting on standby." He pointed to Johnny. "You can come with me. I'm going to have an agent get a formal statement from Laurel and you can't be in the room."

"Okay." Johnny put his hand on my shoulder. "Do you think you are going to be okay for a minute?"

"Yeah." I nodded.

I felt a little better knowing something and someone who had real gun power was going to go down there and figure out what was going on.

When they left, I took my phone out of my bag and dug deep in the bottom for Ben Bassman's business card.

Surely he needed to know about all that was going on. I had to tell him.

"Yep." Ben Bassman definitely didn't have manners like a southern gentleman. Especially when he answered the phone.

"Ben," I gasped. "Listen carefully because I'm at the FBI in downtown Louisville waiting to give a statement."

"You are where?" Ben frantically asked.

"I said to listen, Trixie is missing. Jax Jackson is missing. I know Trigger has her and I can't find Derek. My friend Johnny knows Mike Florenza with the FBI and he took me here to tell them what was going on."

"Laurel, you listen to me." Ben was all calm, cool and collected which pissed me off. How could be so together at a time like this? "Did they record your statement?"

"Yes."

"Do what I'm saying." He gave demands. "Take the recorder if you can get your hands on it and get out of there."

"What? Are you crazy?" I asked.

"Is your car there?"

"Yes."

"Laurel, I know what I'm doing. Go get in your car and meet me on the docks by Porty Morty's. I have guys who can fix this. The less the FBI is involved with your situation, the better."

"But—"

"There is no but about it. Do it!" he screamed.

The phone went dead before I could protest. Something in his voice told me to go. And go now.

I took the tape recorder like he said and put it in my bag. Slowly I got up and tiptoed to the door. I cracked the door and looked out. No one was there so I bolted to the right where there was an exit stairs sign.

I ran down the couple flights of stairs and pushed open the exit door. To my luck, it was on the corner of the building and I could see my car across the street.

Beep, beep.

"Watch out!" A guy screamed out his car window when I bolted across the street and he almost hit me. "You are going to get killed!"

I threw my finger in the air. "Trust me! I know that asshole! Either by you or Trigger!"

I jumped in my car and squealed out of the parking spot, tearing out in front of a car that had to swerve from hitting me.

There was no slowing down. I had the Old Girl speeding as fast she could go, ripping through every single curve.

It only took me fifteen minutes to get back to the docks, but Ben wasn't there. I parked my car on the side of the building next to the dumpster. I grabbed my gun and Trixie's knife from the glove box before I got out.

My adrenaline was pumping and there seemed to be no stopping my feet once they hit the ground.

I put the knife in my back pocket once I reached the side door of the warehouse. I heard someone talking and I peeked around the corner to the boat dock. Jennifer was on the dock having a heated conversation with Trigger. So heated that she smacked him and he smacked her back making her fall flat on her ass.

She was crying holding her face and he spat on the ground next to her screaming something that was inaudible. I didn't have time to worry with him because if he was out here, then he wasn't in there.

"Laurel! What the hell are you doing?" Johnny was standing behind me getting out of a blue Crown Victoria.

"Who's car?"

"You left so quick, Mike let me take his car. They FBI is on the way." He grabbed my hand. "Please tell me you aren't going in there."

"I am and you are either with me or against me," I warned.

"I'm with you." He opened the door and looked both ways before we darted in.

"Follow me. I know this place like the back of my hands." Which had to be an upside to working there for so long.

The entrance we went in was where the extra porta-lets were kept behind a chained wall. There was a little rustling around and if this wasn't going on, I'd have thought it was a mouse, but I had to check it out.

"Shh." I put my finger up to my lip and grabbed the set of keys off the hook to unlock the padlock for the gate.

I had no idea why Morty kept the keys hanging right there if he didn't want anyone to get in the chained area, but that was Morty for you.

We walked up the rows of unused potties until I heard a grunt coming from one of them. I opened it.

"Trixie," I gasped when I saw her gagged and bound to the sanitizer dispenser that was attached to the plastic wall. There was a beating coming from the potty next to Trixie. "Johnny, you help her."

I opened it and Louie was stuffed in there like a little pig in a blanket. He had tears streaming down his face.

"No! Not my finger!" I heard Derek scream in the distance.

"Johnny, help them." I didn't wait for his response when I ran out of the chained area and down the dark corridor leading into the open warehouse where I thought I heard Derek screaming from.

With the gun and one bullet held out in front of me, I slowly turned the corner. There was some big guy with a tied-up Derek, Morty, and Jax. In front of them was a large fish tank that had never been there before. Next to the fish tank on the ground were the two Styrofoam boxes that I had seen Nicoli give Morty on the dock that day.

The big guy was dipping a net in the Styrofoam container and taking out piranhas and putting them in the larger tank.

"I think you are first." The big guy cackled with a big grin on his face looking straight at Morty.

He was obviously taking pleasure from taunting Morty. There was sweat dripping off of Morty's bald head.

"Please not my hand." Morty begged and wiggled around in the rope that he was all bound up in when the big guy approached him.

In horror, I stood there with my mouth open watching as the big guy hooked Morty to the port-a-let lifting crane that we used to get the potties on the truck bed for delivery. Just like an unsteady port-a-let, Morty was hoisted into the air. The big guy untied Morty's right arm and held his hand over top of the tank, giving the crane operator the go ahead to lower.

The guy's hand glistened with one of the Cardozza family's rings that looked a lot like mine. Slowly they lowered and lowered Morty.

Jax and Derek squirmed. Jax saw me and profusely shook his head for me to go back. But I couldn't stand it.

"Hold it right there or I will shoot!" I took a step and stumbled over a walnut.

The gun went off and the bullet ricocheted into the warehouse rafters, landing on one of the unopened crates that filled the space. I fell to the ground as the big guy let go of Morty. Morty's body swung around and around. My body swung around when the big guy grabbed me, but not before first grabbing my gun.

"Well, well." I winced when he picked me up by my forearm and jerked me over to the group. "Look what we have here. A girl." He flung my arm toward the tank. "I bet they would love to have a taste of you." His evil smile exposed a mouthful of rotted teeth.

He grabbed a rope and tied my legs together with my hands.

"I will take care of you in a minute." He went back over and grabbed the twirling Morty.

I looked around and saw someone moving in the shadows. When they quickly moved into the sunlight darting in from the warehouse windows, I could tell it was Johnny.

Thank God. I took a deep breath so thankful Johnny was there, giving me a little hope. I looked for Trixie, but I bet he had gotten her and Louie to safety. Plus the FBI was going to be there any minute. I had hoped they had gotten there and took Jennifer and Trigger into custody. But that hope quickly shattered when he came traipsing in with her on his arm.

"No!" I screamed when Johnny dipped out of the shadow.

I wanted to warn him to stay there so he could watch for the FBI and not get taken by Trigger and one of his men.

"Shut up, Laurel!" Johnny ordered. "Tony meet Laurel London."

"Hey, why is she tied up?" Trigger asked with a questioning look on his face.

"Let me introduce you to The Gorilla's granddaughter." Johnny kicked my foot, causing me to tumble over on my side since my feet and hands were bound up.

"Shit. I knew you were no good Johnny Delgato!" I spit at his feet.

"Bitch." He grunted.

It wasn't him that I was worried about. It was Trigger who was walking over to me. When he bent down to get a good look at me, his knees cracked.

"Well well." He grabbed my forearm and pulled me up back on my butt. "Laurel London were you getting a little kick out of playing me for a fool this whole time as you were driving me back and forth to this shit hole?"

"Don't worry Trigger." I smiled. "Mike Florenza will be here any minute to arrest you and you." I glared over at Johnny.

"Yeah, I'm already here and I didn't call for any back up." Mike appeared out of the shadows of the warehouse. "We all kind of," he waved his gun in the air, "work together."

"Yeah." Trigger laughed looking around at his little posse. "Me, Johnny and Mike met in college. I think it was fate that Johnny lived near Louisville. So I sweetened the pot for him and Mike."

"What are you talking about?"

"Going into the FBI was my dream job. And if I could work for the mob with my FBI cover and make ten times more money…" He winked. "You bet ya."

"And when Tony told me about his family and he was looking for an orphan—and since I'm such a nice guy—he offered to front my phone business and supplement my income if I helped figure out just where The Gorilla's grandchild was located." Johnny walked closer and bent down next to Trigger. He ran his hand down my cheek and stopped them on my lips. "Only I didn't know that it was hot, hot, Laurel London who I had been trying to get my hands on all of these years."

I snapped my teeth at him making him jump up.

Johnny stood up with a grin on his face. He adjusted his pants.

"Funny how you always thought you were better than me, you orphan rat." His nose snarled. There was an evil look in his eyes.

I looked away. Jax had his head down. I could see he was trying to get free while all the attention was on me. Jax and Derek exchanged a few looks while Morty was bawling still hanging and twirling around from the crane.

"Where's Trixie?" I asked stalling for time.

"That old crazy bat," Johnny laughed. "I will take care of her after I take care of all of you."

"Now, let's get on with this." Trigger leaned closer to me and whispered, "This can all go real smooth if you tell me where my ring is. Please don't make me hurt you."

"What ring?" I asked, pretending to be ignorant.

"This ring, bitch!" He jabbed his hand, minus the finger, in my face.

The family ring was wedged on his middle finger.

There was a rustle behind one of the unopened crates.

Without warning, Johnny pulled a gun from his waistband and shot at it. The crate popped open, the door of a brand new port-a-let swung open and hundreds of AK-47 machine guns fell on to the ground.

"You idiot." Trigger shook his head.

Trigger motioned for Jennifer. Without her even asking for instructions, she rushed over and started to pick up the guns like she had done this several times before.

A walnut rolled across the floor without them seeing and right into my reach.

"So," I blurted out to get them to look at me. I wiggled around like I was trying to get free when I was really trying to get my hands on the damn walnut. "You are also smuggling illegal firearms? Morty?" I looked at Morty in disgust.

I couldn't believe he put Walnut Grove in danger.

"Aren't you just a smart one?" Trigger gave the crane operator a nod. "I take any opportunity I can when it comes to business. And I want to thank you for coming to New York where Jennifer owns the agency that is promoting The Underworld Music Festival. Not only was I looking for you in this area, but I was looking for a nice little out-of-the-way location to bring in the last shipment I will ever have. Because with my ring that you are going to give me, I will retire and no one, not even Jax Jackson will be able to find me." He looked at Jax. "My bad." Trigger grinned. "You will be with your little partner. Dead."

When he looked at Jax, I extended my arm to get the walnut and fell over, giving me just the right reach to grab it. Using my elbows, I hoisted myself up while Trigger held a crying Morty's hand right at the top of the water of the fish tank. The piranhas were going crazy. The water was bubbling at the top and you could barely see them.

"My babies are hungry. I'm glad because I haven't fed them in a couple of days." Trigger was giddy with pleasure on the torture he was about to bestow upon us.

Derek caught my attention. He smiled knowing I had gotten a walnut. He nodded toward his hands that he had unbound but were still together, holding the illusion he was tied up. He looked me straight in the eyes. We could always tell what the other was thinking. He was telling me to wait for his cue and hurl the walnut at one of Trigger's men. But who?

With not a lot of time to spare, I slipped the knife out of my back pocket and slowly used the blade to saw the rope in two pieces, leaving my hands free to throw that walnut.

In a flash, Derek jumped up. I hurled the walnut at Johnny who was running toward Derek, knocking his ass out flat…again.

The big guy rushed Derek as I took the knife to cut the ropes that had Jax tied. I put the knife back in my pocket.

Jax tackled Trigger when he noticed Derek beating the crap out of the big guy. That was short lived when Jennifer pulled out a gun which none of us seemed to have.

"Hold it right there!" she screamed firing a shot into the air.

Trigger used the back of his hand to wipe the blood off his lip where Jax had punched him. He took the gun from her after he smacked her ass and planted a kiss on her lips.

"That's why I have a side piece." He wiggled his brows looking at me. "Now, let's get this settled and then I'll dump all of your chopped-up body parts in my tank." He walked over to me. He slid the butt of his hand gun down my face. "Where is my ring? I'm not playing games."

Out of nowhere a barrage of walnuts came flying through the air hitting Trigger in the head while another hit Jennifer along with the big guy, knocking them out cold. The crane operator jumped down just as the warehouse doors flung open and an army of FBI agents stormed in with big black bulletproof vests on and shields covering their faces.

"Jax Jackson." The lead FBI guy walked up to Jax and shook his hand. "I see you had this all under control."

Trixie, Louie and Ben Bassman stepped out from behind one of the other unopened crates that had to be filled with all the illegal firearms Trigger was trying to smuggle. Trixie ran over to me, with Ben Bassman on her heels but he stopped at Trigger's unconscious body first.

"Good throw." I smiled, embracing her and ignoring whatever Ben was doing.

"Do not say a word about the ring," Ben whispered after he wrapped his arms around Trixie and me like we were one big happy family. “Let me take care of that. It’s what The Gorilla has paid me to do all these years.”

“Excuse me, Laurel?” The FBI guy walked over, breaking up Trixie, Ben and my little hug session. “I was the agent at the desk when you and Mr. Delgato came in to see Mike.” He pulled out a tape recorder from his pocket and pushed the button to record. “The FBI had been investigating Trigger Finger Anthony Cardozza for years. We knew there was an FBI inside agent informant that was working with Trigger, we just didn’t know who. So when you came in today, telling me about all of this crazy stuff and you mention Jax, I knew you were telling the truth.”

I inhaled knowing we were all going to be okay.

“Jax has been great. He totally deserves a raise.” I ran my hand down Jax’s arm when he walked over.

“That’s just the thing.” The FBI agent gave Jax a sideways glance. “Jax was removed from the agency when he just wouldn’t let the death of Lance go. He had been placed on our watch list because he has been traveling around watching Trigger.”

“I was going to kill him.” Jax lowered his head. “I couldn’t let the FBI ignore what Trigger had done to my partner. He had a family. A wife. Kids." His voice cracked. "I had to get Trigger back."

"You knew what was at stake," the agent warned. "And how you went about this wasn't the right protocol."

"Screw protocol." Jax spat. "We got him now. And it was my way."

"I'm not saying you weren't right, but it wasn't the best way." They argued back and forth.

"Listen, I just want to get Trixie home. I don't want to stand here seeing who has a bigger penis by right and wrong." I made myself very clear.

"I'm going to need a cut-and-dry statement from you. Can you be at the agency tomorrow morning?" He pulled out his card.

I looked over at Trigger who was coming to and being carted off by a few agents… at gun point.

"Yeah, my calendar just opened up," I said knowing I wasn't going to be going to the Airport Hotel anytime soon.

## Chapter Twenty Three

"Congratulations to you and Jimbo." I sat down next to Susie Warren, Sheriff Jimbo Warren's wife.

Hhmph. She growled staring straight ahead as we and the entire town of Walnut Grove sat in the town square watching the public ceremony of Jimbo's retirement.

After the whole gun-smuggling-mob thing at Porty Morty's, Jimbo felt like it was time to retire, not making a happy marriage for him and Susie since she was going to have to keep her indiscretions even more on the down low, but I didn't have a monkey in that circus so I kept my mouth shut.

I was also glad to know that Carmine was ill the day the Trigger and his cartel had taken over the warehouse. It would have been one more thing for me to worry about. Morty Shelton had been just an innocent bystander in the whole thing. He claimed Jennifer came in to talk to him about the festival and after getting through a few meetings with her, that was when she informed him they were going to be using his warehouse to smuggle the illegal arms and if he didn't cooperate, people were going to die. Plus they were going to pay him handsomely for the use of the onetime smuggle. According to Morty, he wasn't going to go through with it, but I wasn't so sure since I had heard he was having money issues. Still, I didn't say anything because it all seemed to be over and Porty Morty's was back in business.

As far as my whole family history of sickness, well Ben Bassman assured me there was nothing to worry about because everyone was completely healthy in my family, other than death by gun shot.

Of course I wasn't able to tell anyone about it, other than Trixie because she was in on it. Derek and Jax had no idea I was The Gorilla's granddaughter. When Jax asked me about Trigger's allegations that I was, I laughed it off. Trigger also demanded his ring back, but no one knew anything about a ring. Well…hardly anyone.

Not only was Jimbo retiring, Derek was starting his career as a deputy sheriff. Now with the sheriff's job opening, I had to wonder who was going to fill it.

"Why can't it be a peaceful day?" Gia asked and sat down next to me.

She pointed over to the camera crew that hadn't left since Trigger went into custody. The world just couldn't believe that little ole Walnut Grove, Kentucky was the scene for the mob to smuggle arms.

Come to think about it, it was perfect. No one would suspect a shipment to a port-a-let company where there was a river for transportation. Trigger had planned it all out for years. No doubt I had been on his radar since he met Johnny. His wheels had been turning.

“So what do you think they are going to do to Johnny?” Gia nudged me.

“I have no idea.” My attention turned to the camera crew when I saw them stop Jax Jackson.

He stopped and sat his suitcase on the ground. He was going to meet me at the ceremony and then after I was going to give him one last ride back to Louisville to catch his plane to New York.

The agency had cleared him to come back to work. I was going to miss looking at his handsome face and hot body, but I guess I would live.

“Too bad he’s leaving. He’s hot.” Gia nudged me again. “But I do have a new guy to fix you up with,” she chomped.

“No thanks.” I got up and walked over to see what Jax was saying to the reporter.

It looked like he was giving an interview or something. Derek walked up next to him. I had to laugh because he wanted his ten minutes of fame.

"What is next for the new deputy in town?" the reporter asked Derek and stuck the microphone into his face.

"I was hoping to get my new boss in his uniform." he smiled, taking the camera off of Jax.

"Who is the new sheriff of Walnut Grove?" the reporter asked.

"The city would like to offer it to Jax Jackson if he'd like to stick around." Derek stuck his hand out to him to make a good southern gentleman agreement.

"I…" Jax seemed to be speechless.

My heart nearly dropped into my toes when he looked at me with those deep hazel eyes. His mouth opened into a wide grin. He turned back to the camera.

"I appreciate that, but I think I'm going to stick around and open a private investigation service," he said into the camera before he slid his eyes over to me.

"What was that?" Gia asked, craning her neck toward Jax Jackson who was still staring at me.

"I have no idea, but I don't want him sticking around here," I said.

"Laurel London. I think you might have a little crush on him." Gia tugged on the gum in her mouth with her finger before she wrapped the gum around it a few times.

"I don't think so." I glared at him because he would be the first person to hold something over my head if things went south. "Besides. I have a new house to fix up."

When I had gotten Trixie settled back into her house the day of the warehouse takedown, I had gone home where Ben Bassman was waiting for me with Trigger's ring. He had taken it off Trigger's hand when Trigger was knocked out on the warehouse floor from the walnut Trixie had thrown at him. Ben informed me that since I had both rings, I was now the legal recipient of my first installment of The Gorilla's money. That installment was one million dollars with more installments to come.

After he had to pick me up off the floor and through my tears, I looked around the little efficiency. Henrietta and I needed more room, so I put her on her leash and marched over to Friendship Baptist Church. I gave Pastor Wilson a piece of my mind and told him I didn't need his broken down efficiency.

I told Ben Bassman that I wanted to buy the orphanage house with my money only for him to tell me that I already owned it. The Gorilla had established the orphanage in Walnut Grove when I was a baby and it was to remain open until I turned eighteen. In fact, Ben Bassman paid all the bills on it on behalf of my grandfather, which kept it in good standing with the utilities and taxes. I also told him to put the house up for sale in Louisville because I wasn't moving there. Walnut Grove had become my home.

Henrietta and I moved in the next day. Trixie put her little cottage up for sale when I begged her to come live with me and we'd move her chickens too. She agreed and over the past few days we had been spending a little of my money fixing the place up with new furniture. Of course we had to tell everyone in Walnut Grove that Trixie came into some inheritance and bought the place so we didn't reveal that I was wealthy.

"Maybe he can give you a job because you are going to need one if you keep spending money on that dump you bought when you lost your mind." Gia shook her head. "I've gotta go." She made kissy noises when she saw Jax walking toward us.

"Shut up." There was no way Jax Jackson and I were going to get together.

He said a couple of words to Gia and walked up next to me. His dark eyes set along with his strong jaw line. There was a determined look on his face. A look I had seen when he talked about Trigger Finger.

"A private investigation company?" I asked, breaking the tension between us.

"Yeah." He shrugged. "Why not?"

"Oh-kay." I wasn't sold on the whole idea because I never knew Walnut Grove needed a private investigator. Unless Jimbo Warren was the first client when he gets wind of Susie's little indiscretions.

"I want to open a private investigation company and work with the FBI on the side." He stopped and rocked back on his heels when Pastor Wilson and Rita walked by.

He smiled at them, they smiled at him, they snarled at me.

"Still not friends?" Jax asked.

"Not so much. Past is in the past," I added.

"Which brings me to my next bit of business." Jax folded his arms and we looked on as the line was forming to congratulate Jimbo and Susie who were standing at the foot of the gazebo where the retirement ceremony had taken place. "You seem to have all sorts of criminal talents. And thinking like a crook is crucial in the P.I. business, so I'd like to give you a job helping me. Plus I bet you could use the money."

"So you are telling me you want me to continue to help with cases?" I asked and avoided the whole money thing.

He nodded. "Not all cases, but if I need to pick your brain. You know this area and you might be able to help."

"It's going to have to take a back seat to my new cab business," I stated.

"Cab business?" He asked with a sarcastic tone and then laughed in my face.

"Why not?" I folded my arms and shifted to my left to get a good look at him. "I was pretty damn good at it when it wasn't legal."

"Fine." He put his hands in the air as if he was defeated. "So can I count on you if I need some information about locations, people and stuff?"

"Sure." I stuck my hand out to shake on it.

Jax Jacksons stuck his hand out.

My heart quickened when his gaze softened.

Oh no. I jerked away. His shit-eatin' grin widened.

"See you around, Laurel." He winked. "I look forward to working with you."

"If I have time," I quipped.

I couldn't help but watch Jax Jackson walk away. Unfortunately, the pit in my stomach told me that going on the up and up was almost going to be impossible for me to do.

## About The Author

Tonya has written over 15 novels and 4 novellas, all of which have graced numerous bestseller lists including USA Today. Best known for stories charged with emotion and humor, and filled with flawed characters, her novels have garnered reader praise and glowing critical reviews. She lives with her husband, three teenage boys, two very spoiled schnauzers and one ex-stray cats in Northern Kentucky and grew up in Nicholasville. Now that her boys are teenagers, Tonya writes full time but can be found at all of her guys high school games with a pencil and paper in hand. Come on over and FAN Tonya on Goodreads.

Praise for Tonya Kappes

"Tonya Kappes continues to carve her place in the cozy mystery scene with the witty and endearing Ghostly Undertaking set in a small town that is as fun as it is unforgettable."
New York Times bestseller Dianna Love

"Full of wit, humor and colorful characters, Tonya Kappes delivers a fun, fast-paced story that will leave you hooked!"
Bestselling Author, Jane Porter

"Fun, fresh, and flirty, Carpe Bead 'Em is the perfect read on a hot summer day. Tonya Kappes' voice shines in her debut novel." Author Heather Webber

"I loved how Tonya Kappes was able to bring her characters to life." Coffee Table Reviews

With laugh out loud scenes and can't put it down suspense A Charming Crime is the perfect read for summer you get a little bit of everything but romance. Forgetthehousework blog

## Also by Tonya Kappes

**Young Adult Paranormal Mystery**

Tag. . .You're IT

**Women's Fiction**

Carpe Bead 'em

**Olivia Davis Paranormal Mystery Series**

Splitsville.com

Color Me Love (novella)

Color Me A Crime

**Magical Cures Mystery Series**

A Charming Crime

A Charming Cure

A Charming Potion (novella)

A Charming Wish

A Charming Spell

A Charming Magic

**Beyond The Grave Series**

A Ghostly Undertaking

**Grandberry Falls Series**

The Ladybug Jinx

Happy New Life

A Superstitious Christmas (novella)

Never Tell Your Dreams

**A Divorced Diva Beading Mystery Series**

A Bead of Doubt Short Story

Strung Out To Die

Crimped To Death

**Small Town Romance Short Story Series**

A New Tradition

The Dare Me Date

**Bluegrass Romance Series**

Grooming Mr. Right

Taming Mr. Right (August 2014)

**Non-Fiction**

The Tricked-Out Toolbox~Promotional and Marketing Tools Every Writer Needs

Edition: June 2014

Made in the USA
Monee, IL
22 May 2020

31644140R00167